A HOME ON MY HANDS

A Home on my Hands

Elizabeth Lawrence
with illustrations by Lesley Bellamy

The Book Guild Ltd.
Sussex, England

This book is a work of fiction based on fact. No resemblance is intended between the characters and any real persons, either living or dead.

This book is sold subject to the conditions that it shall, by way of trade or otherwise, be lent, re-sold, hired out, photocopied or held in any retrieval system or otherwise circulated without the publisher's prior consent in any form of binding or cover other than that in which this is published and without a similar condition including this condition being imposed on the subsequent purchaser.

The Book Guild Ltd
25 High Street,
Lewes, Sussex

First published 1992
© Elizabeth Lawrence 1992
Set in Baskerville
Typesetting by Kudos Graphics,
Slinfold, West Sussex
Printed in Great Britain by
Antony Rowe Ltd.
Chippenham, Wiltshire

A catalogue record for this book is
available from the British Library

ISBN 0 86332 786 9

1

The House Agents' Notices dropped through the letter box in ones and twos, in half dozens and in packs. It seemed that there were hundreds of properties that were all exactly what I was looking for. Most of them, it is true, were almost twice the price I had said that I was able to pay, but from the descriptions on the foolscap sheets, the countryside was full of fabulous cottages, gems of English architecture, and residences of character, all outstanding and exceptionally good value. It appeared that the task of choosing, from so much, was going to be difficult.

I began my rounds of visiting, a sheaf of papers in my hand and high hopes in head and heart. No directions were given about finding the places and several times I returned home with 'Undiscovered' scribbled on the paper. Most I found but, after hours of losing my way, I thought I must have made a mistake in the address since they bore so little resemblance to the description.

'Interesting period residence' turned out to be a dilapidated villa in the uglier Victorian style. 'Character cottage, suitable for conversion' meant four walls about to fall down under what was left of a once-thatched roof. 'Range of useful outbuildings' I found to be a couple of lean-to, corrugated iron sheds, holding each other up.

'Convenient for shops and buses' indicated something on a main road, with ceaseless traffic passing day and night and 'Secluded rural setting' described a deserted house at the end of an unmade track on the edge of the moors. 'Fine views from the windows' meant you could see something if you leant far enough out, upstairs, looking between the chimneys of the houses opposite, while 'Charming garden, with splendid possibilities for the landscaper' was a clear warning that it had lain untouched for years.

I gradually learned to translate this language and to set out with ever less and less expectation. Even so, the search became more and more depressing and I began to sicken of the sight of half-dilapidated wooden bungalows, their roofs sagging and their gardens high with weeds, or ugly semi-detached villas indistinguishable from their neighbours and began to feel I would never find anywhere that could ever be my home. In this gloomy frame of mind I got off the bus by the village cross in Brockley.

'Can you tell me where Trivetts Lane is?' I asked in the only shop. There was a silence for a moment while I received a peculiar look, the meaning of which I did not realise until much later.

'Turn left at the end of the village, then left again and you'll be in it.'

I said thank you, bought a postcard of the village street and went out. I turned left at the end of the village and then left again and found myself in an unmade lane.

The lane was so narrow that I could almost touch the hedges on either side. The trees met over my head, shutting out the light. Thrushes and blackbirds sang, and drifts of bluebells made pools of colour on the banks.

Beyond the tunnel of trees, framed by the arching branches, stood the group of cottages, their whitewashed walls brilliant in the spring light, that I had come to see. At once I knew that my search was over. I had found where I wanted to live.

I had not expected to find anything like this in a country lane that led nowhere. There were five cottages in the little terrace, their front doors flanked by scalloped pillars and large, well proportioned windows, with leaded panes, that reached almost to the ground. These Georgian façades would not have looked out of place in an eighteenth-century town square. I stood looking at them in a kind of dream.

The lane may lead nowhere in a sense but I soon discovered that it ends in the village tip, bordered by the river. Every imaginable kind of junk is there: old bicycles, abandoned cars, rusty machinery, piles of tin, broken crates, buckets, bottles, rotting mattresses and mounds of

6

Beyond the tunnel of trees . . . stood the
group of cottages . . .

mouldering rubbish, overgrown with docks and nettles and
rank grass, but I knew nothing about that yet.

Now I walked on down the rutted lane, oblivious of the
pot-holes, and stood in front of the cottages. Each had a low
stone wall, behind which were small front gardens full of
colour. There was no one about. Except for the birds and
the rustle of leaves there was no sound, only the quiet of the
country. Here was peace.

It would have been obvious to anyone more practical
than I that there were no drains anywhere near and that the
lane would probably be impassable in winter, but at that
moment I was not thinking of winter or drains.

It was number 2 that I had come to see. I opened the low
gate and walked up the short path to the front door and
knocked. For a few minutes nothing happened. I stepped
back and looked up at the windows upstairs, also well
proportioned, though smaller than the single downstairs
one.

I heard a sound inside and the front door was opened a
few inches. A small, mouse-like woman showed her face
through the crack.

I held out the Agents' sheet.

7

'May I see inside?' I asked.

The Mousey One looked me up and down, glanced suspiciously at the paper in my hand and at last, rather nervously, opened the door wide enough for me to go through. The front door led straight into the living room which was very small, but full of colour from the sunshine streaming through the high window.

'Would you like to sit down,' the Mousey One said.

'You know there are three cottages for sale,' she went on.

'Yes, I was aware of that,' I replied. 'How much are you asking?'

'A thousand pounds for the three,' she said.

I had no intention of buying three cottages. I had scarcely enough money for one, and finding a thousand pounds seemed an impossibility. I wondered, really, why I had come to see them.

'May I look round?' I asked.

The Mousey One led the way out of the living room into a very small back hall. She pointed through a narrow doorway that led from the hall into a room barely six feet square, holding an old-fashioned stained glazed sink and a cooker.

'That is the kitchen,' she said, not attempting to suggest that both of us might get into it at once.

A steep staircase led out of the back hall. I followed the Mousey One up. At the top were two doors, each leading into a small bedroom, the front one looking out to the west, to the hills of Wales, and the one at the back, facing east, looking over the back garden. Here you could lie in bed and watch the sun come up and listen to the cocks crowing in the neighbouring cottage gardens.

After living for five years amongst Lancashire cobbles and wet slate roofs it all went to my head and I failed to notice that there was no bathroom. I said I would come back in the morning.

Next morning I returned, bringing my solicitor with me. His face registered increasing doubt the nearer we got to the cottage, but I was past listening to words of caution.

This time the Mousey One's husband was there and now

I understood why she looked so frightened. He was six foot tall, cross-eyed and red faced. I felt scared myself. We went in and sat down.

'How much did you say you were asking?' I said.

'Thirteen hundred,' replied Mr Thomas.

'But your wife said yesterday . . .' I began.

'Oh no,' she interrupted, with a sideways glance at her husband, 'I said thirteen hundred.'

At this point, I should, of course, have got up and walked out or, at least, continued to press the point, but partly because it seemed a waste of time and partly from an odd feeling of protectiveness towards the Mousey One, who I felt was in quite real danger from her cross-eyed Master, I said nothing. In any case, I was under a spell and could not in any way take the risk of the cottage slipping out of my grasp, so that when the Mousey One came out with the oldest trick in the game. . . .

'There's someone else interested in the property . . .' I fell right into the trap. After a feeble attempt at bargaining – it isn't much use when you really are not prepared to lose – we eventually agreed on twelve hundred pounds for the three cottages, this to include a strip of land further up the lane where I could put up a garage. We agreed on a date when I should move in and off I went. Little did I know what I had taken on.

☆   ☆   ☆

A few days before I was to move in a letter arrived from the Thomases.

'Our bungalow is not yet ready and we shall not be out by the agreed date.'

My furniture was already on its way. I was homeless and I had a feeling that I had to insist that they honour the agreement. I later found that they had moved into a henhouse on their plot of land.

I set off from Lancashire, in my ancient and uncertain car, loaded to the roof line. It was late and quite dark by the time we arrived - Mary had come with me to help me settle in. We jolted down the lane, the car groaning in its springs, and stopped outside the darkened cottage, its uncurtained

9

windows strangely cold and unwelcoming.

I put my key in the lock. It was my own home, the first I had ever had. I turned the key and opened the door.

It was pitch dark. I felt for the light switch on the wall and pressed it. Nothing happened. Mary shone her torch up to the ceiling, to the empty socket. By the light of the torch we found our way to the kitchen. Here was the only bulb that the Thomases had left. Mary removed it and fixed it into the socket in the living room – and we looked around.

I could hardly believe that it was the same place I had seen so short a time before. Beetles scurried across the bare stone floor; strips of wall-paper hung from the damp-stained walls; grey cobwebs hung from the ceiling. I supposed that it had all been hidden by the furniture when I saw it before. I looked at Mary and wondered what I had done.

There was nothing to sit on. We poured hot soup from our Thermos and drank it, standing up. Over the cold floor we spread newspapers and rolled ourselves in blankets. Mary sat up, putting curlers in her hair and night cream on her face. I turned to the blank wall and was asleep before she had finished decorating herself.

☆　☆　☆

We expected the removal van first thing in the morning and I was up early to be ready for it. I have always suspected that removal men travel all night and sleep in a layby and wake themselves before dawn so that they can catch you when it is most inconvenient. At eight o'clock I heard the sound of a van coming down the lane. I looked out. Yes, there it was, rocking from side to side in the ruts and holes, touching the hedges on both sides, like a great Ark, sailing between high rocks. It stopped outside the door and I called up to the driver.

'If you go on down the lane you can turn round and then you'll be ready for off. That'll give me time to get a cup of tea ready for you.'

I watched the van drive on, down the lane towards the dump and then went indoors and put the kettle on. While it was heating up I hastily put a brush over the floors, ready

A large branch appeared to be growing out of its roof.

for the furniture to come in. The kettle came to the boil and I turned it down, ran a comb through my hair and changed out of my bedroom slippers. I looked at the kettle again and found it had gone dry so I refilled it and put it back on the stove.

It came to the boil again, and I turned it down and went upstairs to fold up our blankets. When I came down, the kettle had gone dry again. I was just going to fill it for the third time when I thought: 'It must be at least half an hour since that van drove off. Where can it be?'

I set off down the lane in search of the missing van. Round the corner I came upon it. A large branch appeared to be growing out of its roof and the driver was up a tree, armed with a saw, cutting it off. A group of people, most of the inhabitants of Trivetts Lane, was standing watching, every now and then shouting warnings and suggestions. Two of them had spades and were busy digging away the bank where the front wheels of the van had stuck. Hoping no one had seen me I made off back to the cottage.

Ten minutes later the van appeared outside the front door of the cottage, a nasty gash in its roof and the driver red-faced and not very pleased. He and his mate let down the tail board and started to unload my belongings, still under the fascinated gaze of my neighbours.

11

It is odd how different one's furniture looks out in the road. Chairs and tables and sideboards and beds that look quite nice in their proper places look like an odd job lot from a junk shop. I just wished they would get it all inside as quickly as possible, instead of leaving it all over the front garden and across the lane.

All went reasonably well until they came to the bedroom furniture. None of it would go up the narrow, steep stairs. The driver and his mate lit cigarettes while they stood looking at the beds and the chests of drawers and the wardrobe.

'We'll have to take winder out,' said the driver, as he took his last puff. He trampled across the flower bed and ground out the cigarette end on the downstairs window sill.

Before I could make a comment or protest he had shinned up the stairs and into the front bedroom and, as I looked up, I saw him attacking the window frame with something that looked like a jemmy. In a minute he had removed the entire window in its frame and taken it inside. Miraculously the glass did not break. He leaned out of the small window space and shouted down to his mate.

'Get a bit er rope round that wardrobe,' he called out, 'and we'll 'eave 'er up.'

Helped by one of the onlookers his mate tied a piece of rope around my wardrobe, then: ''Ere she comes,' he shouted, stamping hard on what was left of my primulas.

The wardrobe swung off the ground, swaying alarmingly from side to side across the front of the living room window.

'Keep 'er going,' shouted the driver. 'Give her a shove from under.'

His mate bent down and put his back under the wardrobe and gave it a lift, while the driver hauled on the rope from above.

'She's 'ere' he shouted. 'Come up and give me a 'and to 'aul 'er through.'

The driver's mate left his supporting position below, whereupon the wardrobe dropped several inches, tightening the rope to what looked very near breaking point, and clumped up the stairs. With much heaving and scraping of paint the wardrobe lurched in through the window hole and I heard it drop with a bump on the floor that threatened to send it through the floor boards, accompanied by cheers from the onlookers.

The cheers, however, were cut short and I looked round to see what had happened now. Approaching through the garden gate was a short, stocky man with a very red face, who looked as though he was going to burst. The little crowd parted to let him through and he strode menacingly in my direction.

He had some difficulty in getting his words out, but I gathered fairly quickly that he was the manager of the removal firm, that it was now past twelve o'clock, that, being Saturday, the men were on overtime and finally, that Trivetts Lane was not likely to see his firm here again, ever.

2

Mary had no intention of settling down to live with me. She had her eye on a wider world than Trivetts Lane. The nearest bright lights were sixteen miles away and that was where she was heading, or thought she was. As it turned out things took a different turn, but that all lay in an as yet undisclosed future.

In the meantime I prepared for my lonely life, lonely that is except for my labrador, Samson. I have never been very good at training dogs. I am very conscious of all that the Training Class Dog Ladies say about undisciplined dogs - that it is never the dogs' fault, always the owners' and it helps me to understand how mums feel when they keep hearing the same thing about unruly children. No one has yet written a book about the guilt complexes of Dog Owners. It ought to be done.

Samson was an undisciplined dog *par excellence*. One word from me and all that. He just knew what he wanted to do and did it.

One of the things he wanted to do was to get out when he felt like it. This led to considerable problems, of which more later, but I was very conscious that one of the first tasks I had to do, after coming to live in Trivetts Lane, was to make the garden dog-proof. That meant a fence. Not just an ordinary fence, but a Samson-proof fence. He could easily jump anything less than six foot so it had to be a properly fixed, high enough fence if it was going to be any good at all.

I started by buying several rolls of strong wire netting. I then went to look at the strip of land I had bought for erecting a garage to see if I could find trees to cut down which would provide me with posts. My saw was blunt and I am no tree cutter, so this took quite a time, but eventually I had enough and I set off to dig the holes for the posts round the boundary of my garden.

Mr Thomas has shown me where the boundaries lay. He had taken me out at the back and indicated an L-shaped piece of garden, of bare earth and rough grass, which he had told me was mine. There were no fences or boundary marks of any kind and it seemed as though, until now, there had been free access back and forth behind the cottages, A right-of-way ran behind the last three cottages, by which the occupants reached their back doors. The whole thing was complicated by the existence of a row of privies, one of which apparently belonged to each cottage, to which access was obtained over the seemingly common land behind the cottages. In fact, the privies were no longer used, each cottage having, as a sign of progress, its own Elsan housed in an outhouse, but the ancient rights of access over the land had clearly never been called in question before.

I began on the first hole, set up a post in it and was just stamping the ground firm when I had the feeling in the back of my neck that someone was watching me. I straightened up and looked over my shoulder. A little cluster of people was standing near the corner of the end cottage, watching what I was doing. Most of my neighbours, it seemed, had gathered to see what I was about.

I leant on my spade, smiled and said good-morning politely. I knew that one or more of them must be my tenants although I had not yet discovered who lived in the other two cottages that I had bought. As I should have to collect my rent from them in time I felt I had better establish good relations from the start.

I was met with stony stares and an even stonier silence. I turned back to my post fixing.

'Yer can't put no fence oop ther,' said a voice.

'Oh?' I said, hoping it sounded as though I did not really mind.

''Tain't yer land,' the voice went on. 'It belongs to 'er, that bit does.'

I stopped fixing the post and looked in the direction indicated by the voice. 'Er' appeared to be a little wrinkle-

15

A little cluster of people was standing near the corner
of the end cottage . . .

faced old woman in a dirty raincoat and gumboots.

'Aye,' the voice went on, 'that be Mrs Withenshaw's land, that bit.'

It did not take me long to realize that my neighbours did not agree with Mr Thomas's outlining of my boundaries. I put down my tools and went to see my solicitor.

Fortunately payment had not yet been completed, although the money was in my solicitor's hands. A letter was sent to Mr Thomas informing him that my tenant was disputing the boundaries and that I intended to withhold the remainder of the money until the matter was settled.

A few days later I was alone in the cottage. There was a knock on the front door. I opened it to find a very angry Mr Thomas on the doorstep. He looked more fearsome than before, with several days' growth of beard on his chin. His crossed eyes searched the little living room as he stumped across the threshold.

In a few forceful words he made it quite clear that things were not to his liking but, hoping I sounded a lot braver than I felt, I also made it clear that until he had sorted out the matter with Mrs Withenshaw he would have no more money. At last, to my relief, he clumped his way out, turning as he put his hand on the door, to shout:

'I wish I'd never sold you the cottages.'

Before the end of the week I learned that he had paid Mrs Withenshaw £50 in compensation for the land which he had sold to me, and I completed the fence around the boundary but, for some time afterwards I half expected to see him back, breathing vengeance. I hoped I would not meet him alone in the lane, after dark.

A week later I received a letter. It was pushed under my door and bore no signature or address and was written entirely in capitals. It read:

DEAR MADAM, AS YET WE DON'T KNOW YOU TO SPEAK TO, BUT FOR YOUR INTEREST WE WOULD LIKE YOU TO KNOW THE FOLLOWING JUST TO LET YOU KNOW WHAT A 'DEVIL' YOU HAVE BEEN DEALING WITH WHEN YOU BOUGHT THAT PROPERTY FROM THOMAS. DID HE TELL YOU THAT IT WAS CON- DEMNED? (THE WHOLE ROW IS). ALSO, THE LAND ON

WHICH HE IS NOW BUILDING AND WHERE HE HAS CHICKENS WAS THE GARDENS TO THE COTTAGES WHICH HE TOOK FROM THEM.

WITH REGARDS YOUR WATER SUPPLY THOMAS KNOWS FULL WELL THAT THE PIPES ARE IN A VERY BAD STATE AND WILL HAVE TO BE RENEWED BY THE OWNERS OF THE COTTAGES. THAT IS WHY HE WAS IN A HURRY TO SELL. YOU WILL FIND HIM TO BE A BAD LOT, LIVING ON HIS WITS AND HIS WIFE'S MONEY FOR MANY YEARS. IF YOU WOULD LIKE TO TALK TO THE PEOPLE AROUND YOU WOULD SOON FIND OUT A LOT OF THINGS. WE ARE ONLY SORRY TO FIND THAT YOU HAVE BEEN DONE BY SUCH A MAN. HE CANNOT REST ANYWHERE FOR THE WAY HE HAS TREATED PEOPLE. WHEN HE MOVED OUT OF NO.2 LAST WEEK THAT MADE THE SIXTEENTH TIME HE HAS MOVED HOUSE IN FOURTEEN YEARS. WHAT A RECORD.

THIS IS NOT SENT TO DO YOU ANY HARM BUT TO PUT YOU ON YOUR 'METAL' AND TRY TO PREVENT HIM DOING YOU ANY FURTHER HURT. YOU WILL FIND HE WILL STILL PUT HIS HEEL ON YOU IF HE CAN AS IT HAPPENS TO BE ONE OF HIS TRICKS. HE HAS BEEN THE CAUSE OF UNTOLD SUFFERING AND MISERY TO MANY FAMILIES WE KNOW, OF WHICH NAMES AND ADDRESSES CAN BE HAD, AND, STORIES WHICH WOULD OPEN YOUR EYES. MAYBE WE SHALL HAVE A CHAT TO YOU ONE DAY WHEN YOU CAN HEAR MORE, BUT BEWARE OF THEM FOR THEY TRY TO BE NICE; AS TIME HAS FLED WE SHALL SAY NO MORE NOW, BUT WE WISH YOU ALL THE BEST IN YOUR UNDERTAKING. GOOD NIGHT.'

I put down the letter feeling strangely disturbed. One should, I know, take no notice of anonymous letters and no doubt a time would come when it would all seem hilariously funny, but not now. From what I had already seen of Mr Thomas I could well believe that he was a bad lot and capable of putting his heel on me. I began to imagine all kinds of things that he might do, out of vengeance or just because he was a nasty character. Suddenly it seemed as though a shadow had fallen across the peace of Trivetts Lane. The prospect of living alone loomed ahead.

Were the water pipes about to give us all cholera? The anonymous letter reminded me forcibly that there were no drains in Trivetts Lane. Water from the sink, where I washed myself as well as the pots, ran out into a hole in the back garden. The Elsan, as mentioned before, was in an outhouse, known in these parts as a brewhouse (pronounced brewuss). The brewhouse was actually on my neighbour's land and to visit it at night was a hazardous affair, with always the chance that one might find it already occupied. There was no light inside and no means of locking it. There was an arrangement with the council by which 'the men' were supposed to come and empty the buckets once a week, but the service was highly erratic. Sometimes they came and sometimes they didn't. The problem was, what to do – to dig a hole oneself, or to wait. If one waited too long, it was impossible to lift the bucket.

The row of privies has already been mentioned. Inside were wooden seats and the 'contents' of each privy must, in past times, have been raked or shovelled into a common pit surrounded by a brick wall, which ran behind all of them. Into this pit had gone every kind of household rubbish that could eventually rot down, the whole making, eventually, a rich composty mess which would have been dug into the garden for manure. The other kind of rubbish, of an indestructible nature, was dumped in the garden, and more of that later.

The pit had obviously not been emptied for years and after some weeks of uncomfortable and rather primitive living I decided to send for the Sanitary Inspector. I took him up the garden and showed him the pit.

'I want this cleaned out,' I said.

'You'll have to provide buckets first,' he replied, 'and the men don't like it.'

Ignoring his last remark which seemed to me irrelevant, I repeated my request, adding that I wanted my bucket emptied regularly too. Then I went on to say that I intended

19

to build a cesspit and have a proper water closet.

'Shouldn't spend much on this lot,' he remarked, looking round with considerable scorn at the cottages.

I told him that I had not really asked for his opinion on my property, but would be glad if he would tell me where I should dig the pit. When he realized I intended to do it myself he looked at me as if I ought to go and be looked at, then stumped up the garden to the farthest point from the cottages.

'Here,' he said.

I thanked him, as politely as I could, and he left with a backward glance as if he still did not really believe it.

When he had gone I looked more closely at the spot he had chosen. It was quite six feet above the level of the cottages and immediately under a huge sycamore. I should have to dig down six feet, beneath the roots of the tree, before starting on the pit itself.

I made a visit to the library and borrowed a selection of books about cesspits and how they are made. Apparently there are several variations on the theme. One can have a cesspool, a septic tank, a soakaway or a cesspit proper, with or without drainage. You can build one that is self-contained and must be emptied at regular intervals, quite frequently if you like bathing, not so often if you don't, or you can make one that has holes in it so that the liquid drains away and then it does not have to be emptied for years and years. The question is, where does the liquid drain to? If your land slopes down and your neighbours don't know, it can drain away under their land, but if they do not like it you can be in real trouble.

There did not seem to be much choice for me. The pit would be so far from the lane that I doubted if any emptying machine could get near enough to do the job, so it would have to be one with holes, and that, I thought, would perhaps help to irrigate my neighbours' gardens.

The digging was quite easy to begin with, as the soil was light and sandy, and I dug away for about an hour without too much trouble. Then I hit something. Scraping away with the spade I unearthed a couple of old tins, then three or four more, then a jug without a handle, part of a bicycle and a broken bedstead. I had come upon the cottage midden, full of the rubbish of the last 150 years.

The rubbish layer went down about three feet and then it was sand again. I dug away all afternoon, piling up ramparts on all four sides until I could only just see over the top. The deeper I went, of course, the further I had to throw the sand out, and by the end of the day I was well down, out of sight, with the fortifications steadily rising over my head.

I climbed out and sat down to think it out. A ladder? Terribly slow, and I would probably fall off just as I reached the top. Buckets! That was it! Buckets on a rope. But I should need someone at the top to haul them up. Mary, I knew, would not even want to know. I decided to invite my friends to come and spend the weekend in the country.

Norma was the first, a strong, healthy, fell-walking type. I thought that the country air was just what she wanted after sitting all week in an office. She approached my hole with a wary look and watched with waning enthusiasm as I climbed down into it and began to fill the bucket.

'OK' I called up. 'You can pull it up now.'

Five buckets and half an hour later she leaned over the sand rampart and called down.

'I think it must be time for elevens. Don't you think you ought to have a rest?'

Not unwillingly, but with a sense of a life-long task ahead, I climbed out and went to find some cool beer. Elevenses somehow flowed into lunch, after which Norma stretched full length on the grass and went to sleep. Somehow, no more work was done that day, and, on Sunday, she expressed a sudden desire to go and look at country churches.

When I walked into the office on Monday I found that everybody knew all about it. I quickly realized that it was no good extending the invitation to anyone else from there.

'You know,' said the chief clerk, 'you could be smothered in that hole. I knew a man once who dug a hole like that in sand, and it all fell in on top of him. They took four hours to dig him out, but it was too late, poor chap.'

'You'll have to shore it up, you know,' said one of the accountants. 'That's the only thing to do.'

That evening after work I went round to the local timber yard and asked for something for shoring up a hole, and they sold me six sheets of corrugated iron and eight heavy planks. I roped them on to the top of my old Ford and rattled home up the lane. I had a couple of hours before sunset and by the time it was dark I had pushed all the planks and sheets into the hole and looked down with some pride on my work.

First thing in the morning I went to have another look at my labours. All the timber had gone and three of the iron sheets, and the hole was half full of sand. I admitted defeat and went to see the local builder who agreed to do the job properly for me. He did not laugh at me and was even quite impressed, or pretended to be, by the brick wall I had started to build for the lavatory. It did need a good push to knock it down.

The builder could not start until well into the autumn and by the time the cesspit was completed snow was on the ground. Standing at the sink one morning, enjoying the experience of watching the water run away into my new, real drain, I heard a noise like distant thunder. The cement had cracked in the frost and the roof of the cesspit had fallen in.

3

The builder eventually did the necessary repairs and now I had a cesspit and a proper lavatory I decided I ought to have a real bath. It would be a pity, in a way. Bath time had been quite a ceremony. It had to be planned some time in advance. For one thing there was the problem of water supply. My cottage and the one next door were the only ones in the row that had a piped water supply. The other three, at the far end of the row, shared a communal tap outside the cottage. This acted as the village pump.

All the inhabitants of the lane, except for me and my neighbour with the piped supply, collected there with their jugs and kettles first thing in the morning and exchanged all the gossip. The Queen of the Pump was my Mrs Withenshaw, who knew all there was to know about everybody and held a kind of court there for as long as it suited her. When she had had enough she made it quite clear that the session was over and dismissed everyone to their homes.

The piped supply of water to my cottage and the one next door was temperamental, as my anonymous letter-writer had hinted and, if one of us was drawing off water, then the other could not get any.

I found this out one Saturday morning. I had been busy cleaning up and felt it was about time for elevenses, so I went to put the kettle on. I turned the tap but, after a splutter and gurgle and a trickle of water, nothing more happened. I put down the kettle and went into the garden to collect some artichokes for dinner. This was the only crop that would grow in the sandy soil and it grew with extraordinary vigour. I planted a few when I put up the dog-fence, for a quick-growing screen to give me a little privacy, but before long I found they had practically taken over the garden. Hoping to keep them within bounds I began to dig and eat them, but as fast as I thinned them they multiplied and spread. I became heartily tired of boiled, fried, stewed and mashed artichokes for dinner, tea and supper.

Leaving the kettle I took a bucket and a fork and trudged up the garden. The bucket was soon full and I turned back to the cottage. A stream of water was running under the kitchen door, the sink was overflowing and the floor awash. My neighbours must have finished whatever they were doing with the water and my turn had come.

In time I discovered that Mr Black, next door, was an amateur photographer and when he had a developing day it could be hours before my tap would oblige. Eventually we made an arrangement between us whereby he informed me when this was going to happen, and I told him when I intended to have a bath.

To return to my bathing arrangements. When I could get enough water I filled a galvanized electric boiler by means of a length of hosepipe. When the water was hot I dragged out the tin bath from the cupboard under the stairs and put it in front of the fire in the living room and filled it with jugs of water drawn from the boiler. Then I stoked up the fire, made a pot of tea and put it within easy reach by the bath, undressed, and got in.

Usually this was the moment when there was a knock on the front door which, of course, opened straight into what was, for the moment, the bathroom. If the visitor was female she was invited in and set to work on topping up the bath with more hot water, and asked to pour out the tea. Emptying the bath was a problem which was left to the next morning.

I had to be out of bed early and, hoping that my neighbours were not yet up, I opened the front door and dragged the bath out on to the path, trying not to spill too much of the water on the way, then out of the gate and across the lane to the far side, where the bank sloped down under the hedge. Here the bath had to be tipped up so that the water could run out. I never quite discovered whose land I was watering so regularly.

24

It was all a little public and perhaps there would be a lot to be said for having a more civilized arrangement after all. So the question was, where should the bathroom be? or rather: where could a bathroom be? There were only two possible places: under the stairs – at present dark, damp and distinctly unpleasant – or in the minute six by six kitchen.

I decided on the kitchen; so now I would need a new kitchen. There was room at the back of the cottage to build on an extension. I began to draw plans and work out costs and, when I knew what I wanted, I went to see the builder again.

The plans went through the usual lengthy proceedings of gaining permission and the building began. For weeks the cottage seemed to be swarming with plumbers and carpenters, every room full of planks and tools and shavings and buckets of cement; no taps worked and doors and windows were permanently open, letting in wind and rain.

The men arrived before I left for work in the morning and I tried to find out exactly what they were going to do, but frequently I arrived home in the evening to be met with some completely unexpected *fait accompli*. One day it was the windows. There they were, all fixed in place and cemented in, three feet shorter than they should have been. I hurried down to the builders' yard in time to catch the builder before he went home. He got out the plans.

'Oh yes,' he said. 'They're quite wrong. We'll have to take them out.'

Three days later, the men arrived with the kitchen door. This was to have been glass, to let light into the little back hall, but the one they had brought and were about to fix, was solid wood.

Again I dashed to the yard.

'Oh,' said the builder, 'the men told me you had a big dog and we thought you had better not have a glass door in case he went through it.'

☆   ☆   ☆

Mary took no interest in the question of drains and kitchen-building but she was very happy to join the expeditions to the local, at any time of day or night. The best local was The Anchor, on the bank of the canal that ran through the village. Working boats were to be seen, fairly regularly, tied up here while the boatmen drank and talked in the bar. In the summer an occasional pleasure boat moored alongside, its crew coming in for refreshment after working the flight of locks immediately above.

One day Mary and I had walked the dogs along the towpath – Mary had brought her labrador, Leo, to make her life with me more bearable. Leo was Samson's brother and not very much better behaved.

A pair of boats was working through the locks and behind them came a narrowboat on its own with no butty towed behind. We stopped to watch. The narrowboat had been newly painted and it was clearly not a working boat any longer. Where the open hold had been a wooden structure covered the whole length rather like a Noah's Ark. This, I discovered later, was known as a tumblehome.

As the boat came closer we saw its navigator, a tall, fair-haired man of about 25, skilfully steering from the small deck at the far end.

'Aft,' said Mary scornfully when I referred to it later as 'the back of the boat'.

The boat slid gently in to the bank and the owner/navigator stepped ashore, rope in hand, and tied up. I had never seen a narrowboat close to before. I went up and studied it as nearly as I could without appearing rude. Mary, however, was much more interested in its owner, and when I looked round for her I saw her disappearing into the back door of The Anchor.

I followed and was not surprised to find that she had wasted no time in becoming acquainted with the new arrival. I hovered in the background in my normal un-assuming way until at last Mary noticed me.

'Come and meet Jim,' she said. 'He's going to live here on the canal.'

Jim politely bought me a drink and then promptly forgot my presence. It was closing time before either of them remembered I was there.

Mary walked home in silence, until we reached the end of the lane leading to the cottage.

'Don't you think he's smashing?' she asked.

Samson and Leo were perhaps more surprised than I was to find Mary's sudden eagerness to take them for walks, all of which lay along the canal towpath. I soon became used to the time they were all away and knew that only a small part of it was spent actually in walking. One evening the three of them went out about six o'clock. At seven o'clock I had supper ready. At eight o'clock I ate mine alone. At eleven o'clock I went to bed.

Near midnight I heard the front door open. Samson bounded in and rushed upstairs to my bedroom and leapt on the bed. By the time I had disentangled myself from his flying tail and thumping paws Mary had arrived as well. She sat on the edge of my bed.

'Do you know what he said tonight?' she asked, all starry eyed.

'Of course not,' I said.

'He said –' She broke off. 'You wouldn't understand. You've never been in love.'

'How do you know? Try me.'

'He said he wanted to –' She broke off again.

'Go on,' I said. 'Or do you want me to guess? I can think of lots of things.'

'He wants me to go and live with him.'

'On the boat?'

'Yes.'

'What about the bright lights and all that? Living on a boat is one long chore. You've never done any hard physical work in your life.'

She was not listening. I was wasting my breath.

'I love him,' she murmured, 'and he loves me.'

There was nothing I could do. I turned off the light and went to sleep.

4

The cottage was strangely empty after Mary and Leo left. Samson and I were on our own now. At first he missed his walks to the canal but expeditions to the woods in search of rabbits, or anything that ran or flew, proved nearly as good, but he was an incurable wanderer.

He would be out in the garden with me, to all appearances dead asleep, in a position where he could not move a paw without my seeing. The next moment he would be gone, without a trace. If I went to the gate to call him back I would find an empty lane; not a sign of a dog to be seen and all I could do was to go back and bite my fingers until he returned, hopefully not in charge of the police or bearing a neighbour's hen.

'Perhaps,' I thought, 'he is lonely.' I invited Leo back to stay for a while.

For a time, everything was fine. Leo and Samson raced and leapt all over the garden, breaking down all the plants I had just put in and then tore into the cottage, up and down the stairs and over all the beds, like part of a rugby scrum, their feet covered with black mud.

At last one morning when I was giddy with the two dogs chasing each other between my legs and sending me flat on my face every five minutes, I had had enough. I shut them firmly indoors and went out to work in the garden. It was a particularly beautiful morning and I was soon happily weeding and clearing up, the dogs forgotten.

I finished the border and gathered up the weeds and was just on my way to the compost heap when I suddenly realized how quiet everything was. There was utter silence indoors. Something awful must be happening. It must be quite half an hour, I thought, since I had shut the dogs in. What were they doing?

Dropping my armful of weeds, I dashed into the cottage. No, they were not in the living room; they were not in the kitchen. Upstairs I went, two steps at a time, to the bedrooms. The door of my bedroom was shut. There was no sound from inside.

I opened the door. At first I thought some tiles had come off the roof and that there had been a snowstorm. The room was full of flying white flakes. Then something wrapped itself round my legs. I held on to the end of the bed, unable to move. My legs were entangled in the remains of what had been my eiderdown, a dog at each end.

'Samson! Leo! How *could* you!' I yelled.

The eiderdown whirled out of the door and down the stairs, the dogs after it, in a jumble of tails and legs, followed by a flurry of floating feathers. In the bedroom the feathers were everywhere, spread over the carpet, the bed, the dressing table. As I looked they floated gently down and settled on me as well. Speechless, I shut the door and pounded down the stairs to wreak my vengeance on the dogs.

They were out of sight and I plodded up the stairs again, cursing quietly to myself. I looked again into my bedroom. No, I could not face it, not this morning. I shut the door firmly and went back down the stairs again.

Who, in their senses, would keep two dogs?

It would have been a lot easier if I had chosen another kind of dog. Something small and manageable, like a poodle, would have caused very much less trouble, but I had always imagined myself accompanied by a yellow labrador. Some of its size and dignity, I felt, might rub off on me in some way. At least people would notice my dog, if not me.

One day, when I was walking in the Lake District, I came across a house half-way up a mountain and there, in the garden, was a family of yellow labradors playing on the grass. I leant over the gate and enquired of the owner if he had any for sale. He looked me up and down, staring at my

My legs were entangled in the remains of what had
been my eiderdown, a dog at each end . . .

muddy boots and ending with my windblown hair. What he saw, clearly, did not meet with his approval.

'I do sell them sometimes,' he informed me and then, after a long pause, in which he examined me again, this time from the top downwards,

'The King has two.'

☆   ☆   ☆

A few months later I had been driving through the countryside with Mary when I called out, 'Stop! Look! It says "Kennels. Spaniel puppies for sale."'

Mary stopped the car and we went in.

It would be quite safe, I thought. They would be most unlikely to have any yellow labradors.

The owner met us at the gate.

'You haven't any labradors, I suppose?' I asked.

'Oh yes, as a matter of face we have,' she replied. 'We have just had a litter. Yellow ones. Most unusual. Their father is the local police dog. Would you like to see them?'

The stable where the puppies were was alive with a waggling, wriggling mass of gold and yellow which, as I watched, unravelled itself into seven spaniels and five labrador pups. I noticed Leo first. He was the biggest of the labradors, strong and well formed. I took him up in my arms and stroked him. Just as I was about to say, 'I'll have this one,' I caught sight of another pup, crouching by himself in the corner, his huge, mournful brown eyes saying quite clearly: 'I am an utterly neglected orphan.'

I picked him up, handing Leo to Mary and he grunted quietly inside, rather like a teddy bear when you turn it over. Most of him could sit on one of my hands. Only his paws were enormous, and I knew that I had found my dog.

Mary and I walked back to the car, carrying one puppy each, unaware yet of how these last five minutes had changed our lives.

Leo and Samson slept together that night in a shopping basket.

Before long they had outgrown the shopping basket. We stripped the house of carpets and moved all breakables above tail level.

31

One morning, soon after coming to Trivetts Lane, I staggered down the stairs, still half asleep. It was late and I had overslept. There was no time for breakfast and, forcing my eyes open, I began to search for my shoes.

'Where did I leave them last night? Ah, there they are, under the chair. No, there's only one. Where's the other one?'

I searched under the table, in the corners, under the desk, out in the kitchen. Finally, in desperation, I looked in Samson's basket.

'Heavens! What is this slobbery mess? Was it my shoe? And I'm late already. Who would own a dog, especially a labrador?'

Samson of course, had disappeared on one of his long walks. He would just have to look after himself today. I left the back door open so that he could come in, when he eventually returned, and dashed upstairs to find my only remaining pair of footwear – my bedroom slippers. In these, I padded down the lane to the car, drove to the town and bought myself another pair of shoes. I found some exactly the same as the ruined pair and eventually reached the office rather late.

The following morning I again overslept. I am never at my best in the mornings. I struggled downstairs and groped about for my new shoes. One was by the chair where I had left it the night before.

'Where's the other?' I muttered to myself, my eyes still half shut. 'Oh no, not again!' I yelled. 'That dratted dog!'

There, in Samson's basket was the other shoe, chewed to a pulp, as its predecessor had been. I spread the four shoes out in a line. One right shoe: pulp; one left shoe: pulp; one right shoe from the first vintage; worn but wearable; one left from the second vintage: brand new but, thank goodness, wearable.

For the next five years I went about in odd shoes, but it was better than trying to wear two right ones on a normal pair of feet.

Samson continued to come and go exactly as he wished. Often in the early hours of the morning I would hear him barking at the back door and stagger downstairs, half asleep, to let him in.

One day I was awakened as usual about 3 am. Without opening my eyes I shuffled down, drew back the latch and opened the door. A bright moon came from behind a cloud and forced me to open my eyes. There, on the back step, was what appeared to be a black dog.

'Um, some stray dog!' I thought and was about to shut the door when the dog pushed past me and padded inside, bringing with it a fantastic smell of rotting pond mud. I turned on the light and averted my nose. Along the very top of its back was a thin line of gold. The whole of the rest of the animal was black and stinking. As I watched, horrified, Samson doubled his legs up under him preparatory to rolling on his back for a good dry-clean on my carpet.

'Out!' I yelled, grabbing him by his slimy, evil-smelling tail and giving him a mighty push in the direction of the garden.

Samson gave me a look of grieved surprise. He had never been able to understand the reception he got in the middle of the night. Now, shivering in my night attire, I followed him outside into the moonlight, turned on the garden tap and hosed him down. Ten minutes later I dropped a little sodden heap of clothes on the back doorstep and skipped nakedly upstairs to bed while Samson, now grinning with delight at my discomfort, curled himself into a wet, but slightly sweeter-smelling ball in his basket in the kitchen.

One morning just before breakfast I found that Samson had slipped out. I got myself ready to go to work and then hung about impatiently, waiting for him to turn up.

At last he arrived, a grin on his face, and his tail wagging. There was something in his mouth. He put his head down on the floor and, very gently, laid an egg on the carpet at my feet. Then he looked at me, clearly expecting congratulations and gratitude.

A few days after this, he got out again. This time when he returned he was carrying a chicken. The chicken had not come through the ordeal as easily as the egg had done and was quite dead. I waited until it was dark and then dug a hole in my garden and buried it.

A week later I had a visitor. It was the village policeman.

'Your dog's been caught killing chickens,' he informed me, rather sympathetically I felt. However, he went on to tell me that the consequences would be serious if there was a next time.

What to do? I had chickens of my own that lived on the patch of ground where I had built the garage. There would have to be a sacrifice.

As always, in time of need, I turned to Mr Black.

'Please,' I asked him, 'will you kill one of my chickens, to save Samson's life?'

I went out for a walk while Mr Black selected the wretched victim and executed it. Then I hung the poor bird around Samson's neck in the time-honoured way. He accepted the indignity with his usual tolerance and we travelled like this, backwards and forwards to the office for a week, while the chicken grew more and more smelly. When it got in his way, Samson patiently picked it up in his mouth and carried it, his tail wagging and evidently under the impression that he was retrieving.

At the end of the week I buried the chicken.

'You should write to Barbara Woodhouse,' Mary told me. 'She knows all about training bulls and stallions and undisciplined dogs.'

I did.

'You can easily cure him,' Barbara Woodhouse wrote to me, 'if you have enough determination.'

She gave me full instructions, which I read carefully. I would need another sacrificial chicken. The population of my flock was well down, from natural causes as well as from the attempt to reform Samson, so I went to see the poultry farmer in the village.

'I want a boiling fowl,' I told him, 'and I want it alive.'

The farmer gave me a decidedly odd look, and went off to the chicken run. In a few minutes he was back, holding a large Rhode Island Red by its legs. I held out the cardboard box I had brought with me and he stuffed it in. Holding the lid on firmly, I tied up the box with string and carried it home.

Of course I needed Mr Black to help me once again, and that afternoon we all set off in my car: Mr Black and his wife

Joan, the doomed chicken in its box, and Samson. We were aiming for a lonely common some miles away, but when we got there the common was not lonely after all. There seemed to be a picnic party beside every bush.

We drove round and round until, at last, we found a stretch that was fairly deserted. I tied Samson on to a long piece of rope and we climbed out of the car. I looked the other way while Mr Black executed the poor chicken. Then, following Mrs Woodhouse's instructions, I flung the carcase as far from me as I could.

Samson bounded after it and leapt upon it, wagging his tail at this unexpected afternoon's entertainment. Picking it up in his mouth he came trotting back and laid it at my feet, clearly expecting praise and encouragement. The poor creature was still twitching, as it was supposed to be doing and, again following instructions, I picked it up by the legs and began to belabour my very surprised dog, while all my party yelled and shrieked like a tribe of Indians.

The idea was, according to Barbara Woodhouse, that Samson should think that the chicken was now attacking him and that the shrieking and yelling and general confusion would give him such a fright that he would never want to touch a feather again. Samson, however, showed not the least sign of being frightened. He appeared to look upon the matter as a huge joke, the sort of thing that only mad humans would ever think up. When we had finished he jumped back into the car and sat up on the back seat, a broad grin on his face, and his tongue lolling out.

I looked at the very dead chicken in my hand, and put it back in the box and we drove away in sober silence. I stopped the car by the chicken run by my garage and decided to see if the experiment had worked. Opening the door of the run I slipped the rope off Samson's collar and let him out of the car. He made a beeline for the nearest hen and cornered her, squawking like something demented, while he removed most of her tail feathers.

So much for dog trainers and their theories, I thought, releasing the tail-less hen, which scuttled off into the bushes, still shrieking hysterically. I whacked Samson with his lead, something I had tried many times before, and led him home and put him in his basket.

What to do with the dead hen?

Chicken supper seemed the obvious answer. I invited Mr and Mrs Black to share it and settled down, outside the back door, to pluck and draw the unfortunate bird. This, however, was more than I could take and I had hardly got it into the pot when I had to rush to the lavatory and be sick.

My guests came to supper. They enjoyed the chicken, I believe. I was upstairs in bed, with a glass of warm milk.

The effect on Samson was to come later. Next morning when we went to feed the hens, he took one look at them and then turned round and made off in the opposite direction. Never again did he molest chickens, either mine or anyone else's and when, later, the families of chicks hatched out, he walked round amongst them sniffing and snuffling at them and occasionally helping them to finish up their dinner, and now and then rounding them up when they strayed too far, as though he had been a hen-minder or chicken-shepherd all his life.

After the hens had all died and Samson had passed to the Hounds' Heaven, I acquired a bantam hen with her seven chicks. They had, of course, to be called Sunday, Monday, Tuesday, Wednesday, Thursday, Friday and Saturday. Sunday, Monday and Thursday turned out to be hens and all the rest, cockerels. Two of the cockerels I passed on to friends who did not realize what they were getting and the third one, Friday, stayed to be the incestuous father of future families.

Samson had been succeeded by a Sheltie, named Flicker. Flicker strongly objected to Friday and she was not the only one. The bantams, once they were past the chick stage, were not shut up, but had free run of the garden. Like their predecessors, the hens, they roosted in the trees, and also like them, they made up their own minds about where they wished to nest.

Sometimes I could track them down, or rather up, for their favourite place was in a blackbird's nest in the hedge. This they took over as soon as the birds had completed building and there they laid their eggs. As there were often as many as twenty, many of the eggs rolled off what was by now a platform rather than a nest, and provided some recompense to the birds in the form of uncooked omelettes.

More often, I knew nothing of the nesting arrangements until I saw a little procession of chicks, headed by mum, crossing the garden. Then I had to move fast, to get them into the run before Flicker had a chance to scatter them in all directions. Being a Sheltie, she had a hearty disregard for sheep, but it seemed as though she thought bantams were there for her amusement.

Friday, of course, disdained to go in the run with his offspring. He also felt it beneath his dignity to take off when Flicker started chasing. The hens all rose up, squawking loudly and took to the trees, but Friday just ran a bit faster than usual. Flicker quickly caught him up and, a feather's length away from her, he noisily and clumsily became just sufficiently airborne to mount a low branch out of reach.

Except on one occasion, Friday, more off guard than usual, found Flicker gaining on him fast. Head down and wings flapping he headed straight for the boundary wall. Here Flicker cornered him, unable to take off, and ripped out his tail feathers. The accompanying noise was as when a pig is slaughtered and he emerged from the encounter bereft both of dignity and finery. Friday's voice eventually brought to an end our brief but interesting association. His perch was usually at the very top of a tall cypress from which his exceedingly strident voice rang out over the miles.

One Sunday morning he began crowing about 6.30. I counted the crows and got to 84. By this time I had had enough and, clad in dressing-gown and slippers, I went out into the garden.

'Shut up!' I shouted to the top of the cypresses. There was an instant silence; but not for long. Before I had reached the back door the fantastic noise had started again and continued without pause for another half hour.

Early next morning there was a knock at the front door. I opened it to find a strange lady standing there.

'Good morning,' I said, 'what can I do for you?'

'I live in the village,' was the reply, 'and really I cannot stand it any longer.'

'Stand what?' I asked.

'The cockerel!' replied my visitor. 'You really must get rid of it.'

She was evidently at the end of her endurance and at that

particular moment I was totally unable to think of any really acceptable argument for Friday's continuing presence. She had my considerable sympathy in fact and I found myself promising to see that Friday was sent a very long way away, very soon.

But where?

The friends to whom I had given Tuesday, Wednesday and Saturday had not spoken to me since and I felt I had run out of cockerel-loving acquaintances. Then I remembered the Schools Nature Reserve. Friday would be welcomed there with open arms. What an educational asset he would be!

5

It was not long before Mary and Jim made their union legal. For some weeks after the honeymoon Mary was still starry-eyed and blissfully unaware of the grinding life of a boatman's wife. But Jim did his part splendidly, keeping all the engineering side of things in order, the water tanks filled and the wood and coal and coke to hand.

Seven months after the wedding Mary was rushed into hospital. She returned to the boat a week later clutching her new son. All was well for the first few months, until he began exploring. Then it was all eyes on deck and bi-weekly rescues from death by drowning.

Eighteen months later the family increased once more by the addition of a daughter. Mary approached a state of hysteria, cooking, washing, life saving, educating and trying to remain sane.

'I feel like a mentally retarded seagull,' she said, 'who's built its nest on this cliff and the sea's roaring below. I've laid my eggs and they're going to roll off. Stephen!' she yelled. 'Where *is* he?'

She raced to the far end of the boat and pushed her head out of the for'ard cabin window just in time to grab her two year old by the seat of his pants and haul him on board again. With nowhere to crawl except towards the water it seemed as if Stephen's days were numbered and the new baby would be following him soon after to a watery grave.

'The boat people tie theirs to the chimney,' I suggested.

'They'd only hang themselves,' said Mary.

At last she said she'd had enough and one day she screamed at Jim:

'It's me or the boat,' as she made off to The Anchor.

It took them only a week to find a bungalow, safely surrounded by solid dry land.

The boat was for sale.

Mary and Jim's bungalow was not as far removed from being a boat as they had at first thought. It was on the canal bank, close to the flight of locks above The Anchor. Mary was only slightly less hysterical than before in that the space between safety and drowning was now no longer only seven feet, and there was a hope of catching up when Stephen or Jane took off in the direction of the canal bank before they actually fell in, but life was still pretty fraught.

The family had increased again, but only on the edges. They had now acquired in addition to Leo, a Skye terrier named Sally, who immediately got in the family way, a cat called Tom, and three Chinese geese.

The geese were intended to be a cheap form of lawnmower, but it did not work out that way. When they were hungry, instead of systematically trimming the grass as they were intended to do, they goose-stepped, one behind the other, up the steps into the bungalow and did a round of the animals' dishes, clearing up anything left by Tom or the dogs.

The rest of their time they spent walking round in line, their necks outstretched, hissing menacingly at the heels of anyone they were following. If you turned round to face them they would all be looking the other way with a faraway expression on their faces, like three maiden aunts out for a Sunday walk.

At the end of the orchard was a caravan. It had been there when Jim and Mary bought the bungalow and was inhabited by an old woman, whom nobody ever saw. She was supposed to pay a rent, but this was never seen either and when they had been there for eighteen months without a sign of their tenant paying up, Jim wrote to their solicitor and asked him to deal with the matter.

After some time he received a letter from their tenant, forwarded by their solicitor. It read:

The geese were intended to be a cheap form
of lawnmower.

'The reason I have not paid my rent is because of the wild animals they keep. One is a lion cub. I can tell by his spoor, as well as his roar.'

The lion cub, presumably, was Leo; but they never had her rent.

Keeping the garden from becoming a jungle and the bungalow from falling apart eventually became more than Mary and Jim wanted to cope with, on top of the dangers of losing their family in the locks. They decided to reduce the problems of daily living to a minimum by moving into a caravan. The chances that there might be even more problems did not seem to occur to them and they put the bungalow up for sale. They had not yet sold the boat so cash was short. They bought the smallest caravan they could find that would hold them and the animals, but not the geese who had, by now, passed on.

Finding a site for the caravan might have been a problem but I had the strip of land behind my garage which I had haggled over with Mr Thomas and, one day in February, when the temperature was below freezing, a large car arrived at the bungalow to tow the caravan and its contents to its resting place.

Over three miles of snowy roads it jolted and jogged until it turned into Trivetts Lane. Here, where no snowplough had attempted to go, the drifts of snow were broken only by

41

lines of footsteps. The towing car staggered and slithered and the caravan rocked on its wheels, as inch by inch it struggled down the lane. I walked beside it, almost flattened into the banks by the sides of the van, as I tried to hold back the branches that hung in its way.

'Mind the chimney pot!' shouted Mary who was doing an airfield-landing act from the front, with a lot of arm waving and unintelligible instructions. Just in time I managed to divert a low hanging branch before it removed the pot from the roof of the van.

At last it came to rest behing my garage and here Mary and Jim set up house with Leo, Tom, Sally, the children and my chickens whose territory it had been and who viewed this takeover with some uncertainty.

In spite of the fence I had not been able to keep Samson from wandering, and when he was let out first thing in the morning he always found a way out of the garden.

It was often hours before he returned. Most mornings he visited Mary and Jim on his way out or back and before long they hit upon the idea of using him as a kind of pigeon post, so, most mornings, he would appear at my back door with a note tied to his collar.

'Run out of milk.'

'May we borrow some cornflakes?'

'Please bring water,' or

'Not getting up today. Would you do the shopping?'

The chickens acted as an alarm clock for the caravan. I had bought a rather nice henhouse for them, but they scorned to use it, preferring to roost in the trees.

The first night or two I went around the perimeter of the field dragging them down by the tail feathers from the branches where they had gone to sleep, and popping them into the house where they were supposed to be. By morning they were all back in the trees, and before long I realized that I was outnumbered and left them to do as they liked. At dawn they came down from the branches, and began their morning song and scrape beneath the caravan.

When they felt it was time someone was up and attending to them, they walked up the steps and scratched at the door. When, at last, Mary could bear it no longer and got up, they walked as boldly as you please in through the door

42

and made themselves at home inside. Tom remained quite unmoved by all this, as he had learned at an early age that there was little point in getting excited about the things that usually went to the heads of most cats. Mice, for instance, left him cold. He saw no future in mouse-hunting when he could get a far better meal by sitting and waiting for someone to provide it. Stalking birds only gave him wet paws and wasted valuable time that might be spent asleep on a warm bed.

One day he did, in fact, bring in a young rat. He had probably caught it when he was off-guard, rather than intentionally. He brought it into the caravan, hoping very likely that someone in there would relieve him of it. As he opened his mouth to announce his arrival, the rat took its opportunity and scuttled off under the cupboard and disappeared behind the lining board. Tom shook his paws disdainfully as though to disassociate himself from the whole business and hopped on to the bed where, in half a minute, he was nose-in-tail asleep. Sally watched the whole affair, entirely without interest and in the end it was Mary who sat by the hole until the rat came out.

Searching for eggs from my chickens took up a lot of my time. They scorned to lay in the boxes I had provided for them, and found their own nesting sites up and down the lane. Generally I found the nests weeks later, with a hen contentedly brooding a dozen or more. Very few eggs ever found their way to my breakfast table and the hens themselves all eventually died in my arms as I could not possibly bring myself to kill and eat them.

6

Soon after I came to the cottage I was lying in bed one morning, watching the sun making patterns on the whitewashed walls and listening to the quiet sound of contented, country hens, when I heard a cracked voice calling:

'Katleen! Katleen! It's seven o'clock!'

It was Mrs Withenshaw rousing her daughter, who lived in the cottage next to her, and happened in the same way every morning except Sunday. Eventually Katleen appeared, ready for work, and made her way up the lane to catch the bus. Sometime later Mrs Withenshaw herself went up the lane, dressed, as usual, in a long, shapeless grey raincoat and a pair of Wellington boots, and pushing a battered old perambulator. She stopped outside my cottage; by now I was out weeding the front garden.

'Morning,' she called out, 'Lovely, ain't it?'

I straightened up.

'Yes, it certainly is,' I replied, and she hobbled on up the lane behind the empty perambulator.

In about half an hour she was back. She stopped once more, obviously ready for a chat. I went to the gate and leaned over.

'What have you got in the pram?' I asked.

'It's for de pig,' she replied.

The pram was piled high with pieces of stale bread, cabbage leaves and other items of kitchen rubbish which she had evidently collected from various sources in the village.

'I give 'em some lickie taters too,' she went on, giving me a toothless grin. 'They likes lickie tatties, do de pigs.'

Mrs Withenshaw went up the lane, pushing a battered
old perambulator . . .

Feeling unable to think of a suitable comment, I said
nothing and realizing I was not much use at this kind of
conversation she trundled towards her own cottage and in a
few moments I heard a rattle of pails as she spread them out
in the garden and filled them with the contents of the pram.
Then, taking one in each hand, she stumped over to the
pigsty and tipped them over the low wall.

The grunts and snorts that followed this offering indicated that it was appreciated.

From my open back door I could hear her talking, but as
far as I could see, there was no one else there. I walked
round the back of the cottages towards the sty and there I
found her, leaning over the wall and carrying on a one-sided
conversation with the pig, while he enjoyed his dinner. She
turned and grinned at me.

'A bit o' talk do 'elp to fatten 'e,' she said.

☆　　☆　　☆

45

Mrs Withenshaw kept one pig at a time, carefully fattening it on a diet of scraps and chat, for several months, When she thought it weighed enough she sent it to market, and at last the time came for this one to go.

One Saturday morning there was a noise like an old duck-gun being fired at short intervals and down the lane rocked and juddered the ancient motor cycle and sidecar belonging to Mrs Withenshaw's son George. The sidecar had a net over it and in this rather odd form of transport the pig was to take its last journey from Trivetts Lane.

But first it had to be caught.

Knowing that it was likely to be a sight not to be missed I went upstairs and leaned out of my bedroom window, from where I had a splendid aerial view. Katleen, who did not like the pigs, stayed inside out of sight.

First of all George took up his position by the door of the sty, steadying himself to catch the pig by straddling his legs wide apart. Then Mrs Withenshaw, with suitable coaxing words of affection, opened the door. Out dashed the pig, straight at George. George made a grab and missed and the pig charged on down the garden. George picked himself up and dashed after it, Mrs Withenshaw hobbling after him as fast as her rheumatism would allow.

The pig, almost cornered, turned and doubled back, crashing its way through the rhubarb, snorting and squealing like something demented. Round it went again, in and out of the cabbages, the pig – in spite of its fat, doubling quite skittishly from side to side – just out of reach of its two pursuers, its ears flapping up and down and its agonized yells echoing up and down the lane.

Eventually it grew tired and slunk into the cabbage patch. George leapt on it, grabbing one of its ears, whilst Mrs Withenshaw took a firm hold of its tail. When he had got his breath back, George heaved it up in his arms, shrieking and squealing as though it were being murdered, and dumped it into the sidecar. Before it could scramble out again, he whipped the net over the top and tied it down. He mounted the old motor cycle and amid clouds of smoke and infernal shrieks from the sidecar, disappeared up the lane.

Mrs Withenshaw stood sadly watching the departure, then turned round and stumped up the garden. She stood by the empty sty, looking inside and I heard her say to herself:

"'E were a nice pig, 'e were.'

One afternoon I heard the sound of a car coming down the lane. Everybody watches everybody else in Trivetts Lane and outsiders, visitors or newcomers, are subjected to close inspection. Nobody would choose to come down the lane unless they had a good reason, especially in a car. There were only two resident cars, my old Ford and an even older Morris, belonging to Mr Black. The ruts and pot-holes in the lane grew deeper and wider every year and after each journey we found that some new part of our cars had rattled loose.

I went to the window to see who it was this time and was surprised to see a large, highly polished, six-seater limousine, driven by a uniformed chauffeur, making its way slowly and with appropriate care between the narrow banks.

It passed the cottages and went on down the lane towards the tip, to turn round, then re-appeared and drew up outside Mrs Withenshaw's cottage.

In a moment, the front door opened and a figure appeared. Surely it was not Mrs Withenshaw? No raincoat, no Wellington boots, but a neat black coat, straw hat and handbag. The chauffeur opened the door of the car and helped her in, returned to his seat, and drove slowly back up the lane.

This, I found out later, was Mrs Withenshaw's monthly outing. She had, it seems, been employed for years as a housemaid in the Big House in the village and, ever since, the car had been sent regularly once a month to take her to have tea with her old employers.

Looking at the calendar one morning I realized that it was rent day. I had never been a landlord before and I had no idea how I ought to go about collecting the rent, but I need not have worried. Soon after breakfast there was a knock on

47

my back door.

'Will yer come round for de rent?' asked Mrs Withenshaw.

As soon as I had cleared the breakfast things away I walked round to Mrs Withenshaw's back door.

'Come in,' she called from inside.

On the table lay two rent books, one for her cottage and one for Katleen's.

'Yer signs 'em ther,' she indicated, opening the books to the right places.

She went over to the sideboard and took down a pewter teapot and counted the coins it contained, six shillings and sixpence for her rent, and four shillings for Katleen's. I picked up the money wondering how I was expected to keep the cottages in repair on this amount, and signed the books.

'Would you like to see me cut glass?' she asked, opening a corner cupboard. Inside was an array of beautiful Staffordshire crystal. She picked up a small vase and held it out to me.

'That's for you, me dear,' she said.

Apart from the drains, there was still plenty to be done to the cottage to make it habitable. The woodwork of the door and round the windows badly needed attention and I spent all my free moments during the first summer burning off the old paint with a very temperamental blowlamp, scraping, sandpapering and finally putting on a primer and two layers of blue paint.

When the winds and mists of October finally drove me indoors, I started on the inside. The living room was decorated, if that is the right word, with mud-brown paint and red wallpaper. This had to be removed, along with a number of layers of an earlier era and replaced with white distemper. Mary offered to give me a hand. It was one way of escaping for an hour or two from her full-time job of child-minding. She may even have found my conversation a welcome change from the rather limited communications of her young. I was certainly glad of her company again. Her presence made a good excuse for frequent stops for tea.

48

During these she gave me vivid accounts of married life and its problems which took the form of serials, each lasting about ten minutes and ending on a real cliff-hanger as I announced firmly that time was up, otherwise we would both be geriatric before the work was done.

The hall and stairway presented a tricky problem as we could not possibly reach high enough to use the distemper brush in the ordinary way and we had no scaffolding on which to stand. Eventually we tied the brush on to the handle of a mop, dipped it in the tin of distemper and then raised it aloft in the general direction of the ceiling. Our aim was poor, as the whole contraption was quite heavy, and long before it was anywhere near where we intended it to go most of the distemper had run down in large wet blobs on to us and the floor.

Book shelves had to be built next, a new fireplace installed, the concrete floor painted with red tile paint and the old doors panelled with hardboard, all of which we did ourselves, with the exception of the fireplace, which Mr Black somehow found himself doing for us. We had soon found that his heart was as soft as his hands were skilful.

And there were the ceilings.

The cottages had been built in the framework of a seventeenth-century barn. The original beams of the old barn still ran through all of the five cottages, though now hidden by the ceilings. Lying in bed at night, staring above me, I traced their lines.

'They ought to show,' I said to myself.

The first thing was to take down the ceilings in the upper rooms. No problem, I thought, in my innocence. Mary had returned to being a housewife-mum by now so I was on my own again.

I borrowed a ladder. I got it through the back door quite easily but no way could I get it to turn the corner at the top of the staircase. I took it out again and leant it up against the back wall. It just reached the sill of the bedroom window. I went upstairs and opened the window, leaned out and grabbed the lowest rung I could reach and dragged.

The foot of the ladder left the ground. I dragged again, narrowly avoiding putting the end of the ladder through the window pane. Now the ladder swung like a seesaw, half in, half out. Another heave and the top was lurching about inside the bedroom, aiming straight for the mirror in the front of my wardrobe. I gave it a quick steer to the left to avoid the collision.

'Hi!' came a voice from below.

Hand over hand I made my way back to the window, squeezed through the gap that the ladder was not actually occupying and looked out.

'Threepence to pay on this!' called the postman, waving a letter at me.

'Oh heavens,' I called back. 'Can you come back tomorrow?'

The postman looked up at the rocking ladder more in pity than annoyance, threw down the letter in the open kitchen doorway and retreated to safety.

I set the ladder up in the corner of the bedroom. With great care I climbed up, a long screwdriver in my hand. The first blow brought a shower of plaster down on my head. Blinded and choking, I stumbled down the ladder and staggered to the window, coughing and blowing. When I could breathe again I found an old pillowcase and tied my head in it. I climbed the ladder again.

Taking a deep breath I made a second attack. A ripping, rending sound told me I was now into the ceiling proper. Down came the worm-eaten, rotten laths enveloping me in a cloud of powdery dust as they showered over and round my defenceless head. On I went, eyes, ears, nose and mouth full of plaster. Gritting one's teeth had a new meaning.

At last the hole was large enough to get my head through.

Nervously I went up another rung and peered into the darkness under the tiles, wondering what I was going to find. There were no bodies, but a mass of old birds' nests scattered over the ceiling and a dark stain down the side of the chimney, which could only be damp. I came down the ladder.

'How does one stop the rain coming in?' I thought.
'Especially when you've never done anything like it before?'

Next day I bought a bag of cement and dug up some sand from the garden, where there was plenty. I mixed it all up in a bucket and poured on some water.

It did not look quite right, more like thin grey porridge than concrete, but I dipped in my builder'a trowel and scooped up a little on the tip. Balancing it with great care I began to go up the ladder. Before I was two rungs up it had all dripped off on to the floor.

'It must be too thin,' I thought and poured in some more cement. Immediately the whole thing turned solid. I could not even stir it. I poured some more water into the bucket and it turned back into thin porridge. I began to think that building was not quite the easy job it looked.

I repeated the whole process – more cement, more water, more cement – until the bucket was brimming over and it looked a bit more like the real thing. Again I balanced a small lump on the tip of the trowel and made for the ladder. This time I got halfway up. I was just about to slap it on to the side of the chimney where the crack was, when it slid oozily down my arm and into the sleeve of my overall.

Down I came, scraping the lump of cement from my arm back into the bucket. By this time the brimming mass was beginning to set and I was getting desperate. Holding the heavy bucket in one hand and the trowel in the other I pushed myself up the ladder by my stomach, then, balanced precariously as near the top as I dare go, I chucked a large sloppy lump of cement at the offending chimney. To my surprise it stayed there.

Now that there was a hole in the ceiling the problem of getting the rest down was much easier. With my head through the hole I could keep going for much longer without being suffocated by plaster dust, and battering from above the ceiling brought the laths and plaster crashing to the floor in huge chunks.

From above I looked down on the swirling cloud of white dust with some satisfaction and reasonable comfort and, as long as I remembered to take a deep breath before coming down the ladder, I was all right, since it lasted me until I had shuffled my way through the pile of laths to the door and down the stairs into fresh air. Here, in the back garden, I stripped off as many layers of clothes as I could while still remaining decent and shook out the pillowcase I had wrapped around my head.

At last it was done, and the ceiling lay in heaps on the

bedroom floor, but what to do with it now? I shovelled it up into buckets and carried them, two by two, up the lane, where I emptied them into holes and ruts. After twenty-two journeys I stood in the empty bedroom and looked up at the vault over my head, the sky showing through the chinks between the tiles, and the old beam running across from side to side and felt some pride.

Then I spotted the wormholes. The worms had probably been gone for a hundred years but one never knew.

I bought a tin of Rentokil and read the instructions.

'Squirt into every hole,' it said, or something like that. There were at least fifty holes in the first six inches and after meticulously injecting each one of the first twenty, I gave up and took to the paint brush. I felt that the smell alone would probably be enough to discourage even the most determined of worms and I was longing to get on to the job of staining the beam a rich dark colour.

There was no problem about this, except for the splashes. Unfortunately Mary had offered me some of her sheets to cover the floor and they will bear the marks of dark oak until they eventually fall to pieces.

It was now winter and the snow soon found its way between the gaps in the roof tiles and when the snow had gone the rain followed. One of my guests actually put up an umbrella over himself in bed. The new ceiling must be got up as soon as possible. I bought two large sheets of board and dragged them up the stairs. At grave risk to life and limb, I hauled them to the top of the ladder and shoved them across the top of the beam, very nearly falling off in the process. There they dangled, suspended like an enormous seesaw until I could cement them firmly to the top of the walls.

It was then that I discovered the gap. The old ceiling, below the beam, had rested on the top of the surrounding walls, but my new ceiling, above the beam, was about six inches higher and had nothing to rest on. What was to be done? Clearly a new course of bricks was needed, on top of the present walls.

There were plenty of bricks lying about in the garden. I gathered an armful and took them upstairs and mixed another bucket of cement. It was not difficult to fix a new course of bricks on top of the main walls, but two of the bedroom walls were nothing more than lath and plaster partitions with a gap between. I had not reckoned on the problem of laying a course of bricks on nothing.

Balancing as well as I could on the ladder I set a brick in the right position on top of the partition. With a trowel full of cement I was about to fix it firmly there when it disappeared behind the partition. I put another in its place, and that went the same way. I saw myself filling the space between the partitions with bricks for years to come.

After the sixth attempt I got one brick to stay where I put it. I surrounded it with a thick layer of cement and put another next to it. That vanished as before.

I would soon run out of bricks at this rate, I thought, but in time, more bricks stayed up than went down and slowly the row above the partition grew.

At last it was done, and the ceiling boards rested firmly on the dado of bricks. There was nothing more to be done now than to put a coat of white paint on the ceiling, being careful not to mark the beam. I was proud of it.

'All my own work,' I murmured as I lay in bed, looking up. 'I've actually done it.'

7

I had always wanted to ride. As soon as I was old enough to straddle the back of an armchair it became my horse, with loops of string for stirrups. The smell of someone else's leathers had had to satisfy me in my poverty-stricken youth as I trotted on foot behind my wealthier friends around Richmond Park. I did manage to con my grandmother into paying for half a dozen lessons by persuading her that the ability to ride might make all the difference to my getting a job looking after children in my holidays.

Needless to say I never made use of my dishonestly gained skill.

I had two holiday jobs. The first one required me to coach a fourteen-year-old schoolboy in French. We used to cycle up to Goodwood on summer afternoons and lie under the beeches in the cool shade. I then produced the French grammar, but *je suis, tu es, il est* had little chance with the downland breeze lifting the leaves overhead and glimpses of long unbroken horizons showing between the smooth grey trunks.

The other job was with a titled family living on the borders of Wales. I was supposed to coach them also, but again, the project was doomed from the start. Summer holidays, in the children's view, were sacred, to be given to picnics, dressing up and riding (for them, not me. They needed no coaching in that direction); certainly not lessons.

I was met at the station by the uniformed chauffeur and driven the ten miles to the country house-cum-farm where they spent the summer. In winter they lived in a large house near Grosvenor Square.

The four children were having so-called nursery tea when

I arrived, which meant that they could consume large quantities of bread and jam and talk with their mouths full, while their parents were able to enjoy their leisure unencumbered by the responsibilities of their children.

They looked up as I entered the room. If their looks had been capable of bodily destruction I should have dropped dead at that moment. The rest of the holiday was spent in polite rebellion on their part which my continuous efforts at reconciliation failed to subdue.

Their mother, Lady X, was an 'invalid' and spent the entire holiday in bed. Lord X and I were the only other visible members of the household, the servants living entirely behind the green baize doors, like moles and from which I never once saw any of them emerge.

Evenings were spent à deux beside the huge peat fire, Lord X reading *The Times* and taking snuff while I tried to pretend that I was not there. He was extraordinarily handsome and I sometimes think that if I had not been so terrified we might have had an interesting time. As it was, we never spoke a word to each other.

It came to the end of the holidays. Lady X summoned me to her bedside.

'The children have to go to the dentist and have their hair cut,' she said. 'You will take them in the pony trap tomorrow.'

'Yes,' I heard myself murmuring as I backed out of the Presence. I had never driven a pony trap in my life, but I was not going to tell her. We would get there and back, sans teeth, sans hair, if that was the last thing any of us did.

The groom had the pony and trap ready after breakfast next morning and I climbed in and took the reins, trying to look as though this was something I had done from my youth up. All right so far. Obviously the pony knew exactly what to do. It found its way out of the gate and into the lane with no help from me.

'I want to drive,' insisted the oldest of the children as soon as we were out of sight of the house. Knowing she would be better at it than I was I handed over the reins with some relief.

We covered the ten miles to the market town without incident and all was well until we reached the dentist. The children all scrambled out, leaving me to park the pony and trap. I tied it to what I thought was a suitable looking post and accompanied the children to the waiting room. As the door closed behind us I heard a loud crash. I looked through the window and there was the pony with its feet through a cold frame.

I remembered nothing of the rest of the proceedings until the day was nearly over. We were just coming up the home stretch, almost in sight of the gate, when a grey pony with its rider, came trotting towards us.

'Who's that?' called one of the children. 'Never seen it before. Come on, let's go and find out.' Before I could protest, the four children had all leapt out of the trap leaving me in sole charge.

The pony of course trotted into the stableyard with no trouble and then stood still, obviously waiting for me to do the next thing.

I got down from the trap and approached the pony somewhat gingerly. In spite of my strong desire to ride I have always had a love-hate relationship with horses. I have never felt I could depend on them. When, years after, I had a pony of my own, I used to urge it to gallop and then pray that it would stop. There was no one about in the stableyard. The groom had clearly gone off duty. Certainly the pony could not remain fixed to the trap indefinitely, but how did one unfix them?

I started undoing the nearest buckles. They happened to be the right ones. The shafts dropped to the ground with a clatter. At least I had separated pony and trap, but what next?

Pursuing my line of trial and error I undid another two buckles. Something else, for which I knew no name, came off. I undid some more buckles. Then, too late, I found that everything was off! What now?

The pony started to trot. There was nothing to hold on to now, except for its tail or its mane. I preferred the mane, being farther from the kicking equipment. I clung as hard as I could while the pony trotted on, dragging me after it. How was I to know that it only wanted to get back to its field? It was much too valuable an item for me to lose carelessly. I did not fancy having to own up to such a lapse, never mind admitting to a total ignorance of anything to do with horsemanship. The scorn of the children when they found out would be the very end for me.

Fortunately, the pony came to a halt in front of the field entrance and, still holding its mane, I opened the gate. Kicking up its heels it cantered through. I wiped the sweat from my forehead, swept the bits of confused harness into a reasonable pile and disappeared indoors before the children returned. Nobody ever knew the truth.

☆   ☆   ☆

The experience had not taught me a lesson. The urge to ride was still rumbling within and now, here I was living in the country for the first time. Everywhere I looked there seemed to be empty fields just waiting to be grazed and a voice kept popping into my mind at unguarded moments.

'You, too, could have a horse.'

I tried to ignore it. Far too expensive, I told the voice. I would not have enough time, I said. I'd fall off. The horse would get out. But the voice would not be put off and, at last, I wrote a letter to Mr Foot, a farmer in the neighbouring county, who bred horses.

'Have you,' I asked him, 'a suitable horse or pony for an indifferent rider like me?'

He replied by return. He had, he said, exactly what I was looking for.

I drove over the following weekend. In one of his fields was a dark bay mare, half Welsh and half Arab. She looked just the right size.

'We'll catch her,' he said, 'and you can try her out.'

There were several other horses in the field. Mrs Foot came to help.

'Come on, Jenny,' she called as we tried to corner her. It took three of us to catch her.

A remark that the farmer's wife made as we gradually closed in on the pony, separating her from the other horses, came back to me forcibly later on, though at the time I hardly noticed it. I had seen that she was careful to keep out of the way of one of the horses, a tall, handsome animal with a fine head.

'I don't like that stallion,' she had said.

At last the mare was caught. I saddled her, mounted and took her out in the lane for a trot. She was gentle and responsive to legs and reins, but lively enough for me. I rode back to the farm.

'She'll do for me,' I said to the farmer. 'I'll come over and collect her next weekend, if that's all right.'

It was about forty miles in a direct line from the farm to my home but I would have to cross the river that formed the county boundary and that would add another ten or fifteen miles to my journey. It was too far for a day's ride, both for the pony and for me.

'They'll put you up at the Waggon and Horses,' Mr Foot told me. 'There's no need to book. They will have plenty of room.'

The following Saturday Mary drove me over to Mr Foot's farm. We caught and saddled Jenny and about four o'clock I headed out of the farmyard and set off up the lane towards the hills. I had a map with me but I was hoping to rely mainly on a general sense of direction.

The evening sun was warm on my back as I headed eastwards, the stirrup irons felt strong under my feet and the smell of leather and the warm movement of Jenny's body filled me with contentment. I opened the gate into a field at the end of the lane and headed across country. At a touch from my heels Jenny started to trot. The May hedges were bright in the late sun and the blackbirds sang. Everything seemed intensely alive and full of colour and sound. Heaven for me, I thought, would be something like this.

Suddenly I felt a shiver run through Jenny's body. She stopped in her tracks, her ears pricked forward. I looked across the field. Cantering towards us from the far side, his head down, was a bull.

I whipped Jenny round and urged her to a canter, back towards the gate by which we had entered the field. I dug my heels into her sides, not daring to look round and pressed her forwards. I could hear the bull behind us, thudding the ground as he gradually gained on us. We reached the gate. I threw myself out of the saddle, slipped my arm through the reins and with both hands I lifted the gate and pushed it open far enough to drag Jenny clumsily through the gap. I turned to close it behind me as the bull, snorting with fury, pulled up, inches behing me.

Now I had to find another way. I mounted again and followed the lane to its end. Here it became nothing but a rough track, leading upwards towards the hills, with high hedges on either side. The sun was almost down by now and the warmth of the day was going. I rode on. The track became steeper. Jenny's feet slipped on the loose stones while I leaned forward, almost lying on her neck. Now the hedges had gone, the distance vanished and I found myself on an open space above the valley. I searched the gathering darkness for some landmark that I might recognize.

Not knowing what else to do I kept on as straight a line as I could, the only light now coming from the streak of pale sky above the dark horizon. Suddenly Jenny stood still, almost pitching me over her head. I peered into the darkness and was just able to see that her hooves were standing on the edge of a bog. I reined back and started to skirt round its edges, but after I had covered a few yards of firm ground I found myself on the edge of it again. I turned Jenny round, but the bog was now behind as well as in front. All firm ground seemed to have disappeared.

I stood gazing at the darkening land. I could feel the pony's hooves sinking into the mud beneath us.

The darkness came closer. I felt I had never been so alone in my life. Not knowing what else to do I let the reins fall on Jenny's neck, trusting that she would somehow find a way.

Now it grew cold. A chill wind blew Jenny's mane across her neck and I shivered with fear, as she circled round and round, stepping from one foothold to another in the bog.

I do not know how long we continued like this, until quite suddenly the sky cleared. The moon emerged from behind a bank of cloud and a streak of light appeared on the horizon. Silhouetted against it was a group of horses, close against a wire fence. If they had got up there, I thought, there must be a way down.

I gathered up the reins, touched Jenny's sides with my heels and headed her in the direction of the fence. The moonlight was reflected now in the bog water and with the skill of a moorland pony Jenny picked her way between the holes until at last we reached firm ground. Then, keeping as close to the fence as possible, we made our way along through the darkness.

After a time the ground began to slope downhill and I realized that we were at last off the fell top and making our way into the valley. Before long the grass gave way to a stony track and the track to a lane. Then I saw lights and the outline of houses and the incredibly welcome sound of traffic on a road.

Now I knew how tired I was, but I set Jenny to a trot along the high road, to where I knew the inn was on the Ludlow road. Stiff and aching, I slid out of the saddle and tied the reins to the fence outside the Waggon and Horses. I went into the bar. The group of men put down their glasses and stopped talking.

'Can you put me up for the night?' I asked.

'Sorry,' said the man behind the bar. 'We're full, but you'll get a bed in the town. It's only six miles down the road.'

'Six miles,' I thought. He might as well have said sixty.

'I've ridden twenty miles today,' I said, collapsing on a bench. 'I don't think my pony can go another yard, nor can I.'

The landlord looked at me, then he disappeared into the back regions, leaving the locals to stare at me. In a few minutes he returned.

'I've arranged something for you,' he said. 'They'll put you up at the Black Horse. It's only a mile down the road, and they've got a field for your pony too.'

I doubt if I thanked him properly, but got to my feet and staggered out. Jenny had recovered a little with the short rest and in a few minutes we were on our way down the road again, heading for the Black Horse.

Twenty minutes later I was sitting in front of a large plate of bacon and eggs. One of the bars had been made into a bedroom for me and Jenny was happily cropping the grass in the field across the road.

8

Morning came all too quickly and I found, on sitting down to breakfast, that my three hours in the saddle had resulted in a very uncomfortable blister. Worse than this, I realized that now I had to catch and harness Jenny by myself. It had taken three of us to catch her yesterday and, as for the harness, I had only the most rudimentary knowledge of how to put it on. Supposing I could not catch her, and supposing I could not saddle and bridle her?

I packed my luggage, which consisted of a map and a toothbrush, paid my bill, thanked the landlord for all the trouble he had taken and walked out of the inn as jauntily as I could, the bridle over my shoulder and saddle on my arm, trying to look as though this was something I did every morning.

I crossed the road to the field and looked over the gate. Rather to my surprise, Jenny was still there. Pulling a tuft of the greenest grass I could find, I climbed over.

'Jenny,' I called. 'Jenny, good girl, come here!'

Jenny raised her head, looked at me and cantered off to the far corner of the field.

I followed her quietly over the field. She soon had her head down again and was cropping the grass as if nothing was happening, but I could see from the twitching of her ears that she was watching me and that she had already sized me up. She waited until I was almost up to her, then, with a toss of her head, she was away, over to the other side of the field. Again I followed and the process was repeated. It looked as though the chase might go on all day. Then, suddenly, she seemed to grow tired of the game. She stood still and waited for me to come up beside her.

I looked at the bridle hanging over my arm and wondered how it went on. I tried to remember how it looked when it was on, but with all the buckles undone it just seemed to be a meaningless bundle of straps. I took hold of her ears and slipped the longest, loosest bit over her head. Now, what? Which strap went into which buckle? There seemed to be far more loose ends than there had been yesterday.

Jenny stood very patiently while I fumbled until, at last, more by chance than skill, I seemed to have got it right, with no odd ends left over. I slipped my hand through the cheek strap and led her back to the gate where I had left the saddle. As gently as I could I laid it over her back, watching both ends of her rather apprehensively for signs of disapproval, but she seemed to be thinking about something else and made no protest of any kind.

I leant down to gather up the girths below her stomach, still keeping a watchful eye on hooves and teeth. Then I tried to get the straps to go into the buckles. They would barely touch, never mind go through. Had they shrunk, in the night?

Straining and panting I at last managed to get the tip of a girth through one of the buckles. I held on, gritting my teeth. Jenny, meanwhile, was unconcernedly cropping the grass as though it had nothing whatever to do with her. Still holding the end of the girth I glanced across the road, hoping that nobody was watching the performance.

I took another hold on the girth and heaved. Another inch came through the buckle. Jenny moved forward, nearly throwing me under her legs. I heaved again, wondering if I were doing a mortal injury to her. The girth was now so tight that I could not get a finger under it. I stopped for breath.

Once more I gripped the girth and tugged, and suddenly, like a balloon going down, Jenny's stomach deflated. The girth slipped easily through the buckle and I fixed it through the third hole. Then, before she had time to blow herself out again, I fixed the second girth, tightened them both, led her through the gate, gathered up the reins and mounted.

Now I really knew I had a blister. I rode the next six miles in agony until I reached the next village. I tied Jenny outside the only shop and went in and asked for some sticking plaster. A little way down the lane I found a convenient hedge behind which I hid while I fixed the plaster on my sore bottom.

It was dark by the time I reached the field bordering the canal in Brockley, which was to be Jenny's home; and she had cast a shoe. Had it not been for this I should have had no warning of the next catastrophe. There was no forge nearby. Horse and pony owners relied on the services of an itinerant farrier. He arrived in response to my call with a suitcase of ready-made shoes, rather like a commercial traveller. After looking at Jenny's feet, he selected a shoe to fit and lifted her hoof on to his leather apron. With a few strokes of his hammer the shoe was on. He wiped the sweat from his forehead.

'Did you buy this mare in foal?' he asked me.

I stammered some incoherent reply.

'Well, she is,' he said.

I knew little enough about horses and nothing at all about mares in foal. I could hardly have been more surprised if he had told me I was pregnant myself. Later, after he had gone, I remembered what Mrs Foot had said about the stallion. It had been a large, dark Arab, and I guessed that this was all his doing.

Next day I went to the library and borrowed all the books I could find about brood mares and horse breeding. I rang up the vet.

The more I found out, the more worried I got. I laid in stocks of hay and oats and watched Jenny grow larger and larger as the months went by, until I could no longer ride her.

Winter came. The canal froze from side to side. Each morning on my way to work I drove to the field and broke the ice so that she could drink. In the evening I took oats and hay to her and collected her manure to spread on my garden. The car began to look and smell like a farmyard.

Spring came at last. Jenny was enormous and I thought the birth must be imminent. There was an orchard at Mary's bungalow. She would keep an eye on her, and one April evening I led her down the road, hoping we would get there before she gave birth.

Two weeks went by, and Jenny had eaten the orchard bare, but no foal had appeared. I took her back to her own field.

A fortnight later, when she looked like a barrel on legs, I took her back again to Mary's orchard and there, one May morning, under the apple blossoms, the foal was born.

It was a filly, fine and beautiful, with a gentle and lovely head and long delicate legs.

Now they would have to go back to Jenny's own field, for there was no feed left in the orchard. I went to put a halter on Jenny, but she lowered her head and bared her teeth and would not let me come near. I climbed over the fence, holding out a handful of oats, but she whipped round with her back to me, prepared to strike out with her hooves. I retreated with as much dignity as I could and a seemingly insoluble problem on my hands.

'Mr Black,' I thought. 'He'll help. I haven't found anything he can't do yet. I'm sure he isn't frightened of brood mares.'

When I informed him about his latest task he showed no reaction, in any direction. I had come to expect this deadpan expression whenever I came up with anything in which I needed his help. I was not quite sure how to interpret it. It could have been 'Ah, this is just what I was hoping she would ask me to do,' or 'Um, well, it'll be the last time,' or 'Gee, here comes that mad woman again.' I was left to guess, but the fact was that I never knew him to refuse. On the other hand, he did move away about a year or so after I moved in; to Canada in fact.

On this occasion he showed his usual *sang-froid* and together we set out to walk to Mary's bungalow. Mr Black's apparent unconcern about Jenny's temper comforted me quite a lot, but I was still not looking forward to the next couple of hours. Nevertheless I had a plan.

At the bottom of a bucket I put a handful of oats, then arranged Jenny's halter around the top. Holding this in front of me I approached the fence and called her. Ears back and head down she came towards me, the foal following close behind.

I climbed under the wire and held out the bucket. Jenny had stopped a few yards away from me but now, smelling the oats, she stretched her nose towards the bucket. Nostrils quivering, she took a wary step forward, her ears flat against her head. I stood as still as I could.

This was the nearest I had been to her since the foal was born and my first chance of seeing the filly close to. Her delicate head, with great brown innocent eyes, fringed by long, dark lashes, was perfect. Standing close by the mare she rubbed her cheek against Jenny's side as if she were still part of her. Then Jenny moved, the foal lost her balance and collapsed into the grass in a heap of spindly legs and knobbly joints.

Jenny turned to the foal and with her head helped her back on her feet, then she took another step towards the bucket. Not daring to come any closer she stretched her neck until her lips touched the rim. The heady scent of the oats filled her nostrils, and down went her head to the bottom. Quickly I whipped the halter up and over her nose and ears and held on. Up went her head with a jerk that sent the bucket rolling and almost knocked me off my feet, but the rope slipped tight and I held on as hard as I could. She dragged me a few steps along the grass and then stopped.

'Well done!' I heard Mr Black's encouraging voice behind me. 'I'll open the gate and you can lead her through.'

It all seemed too easy. No broken bones; no one thrown through the hedge or swung off his or her feet, not even a nip or a bruise. Looking at Jenny, walking quietly beside me, with the filly trotting along beside her, I thought: 'I wonder what the next problem is going to be. It must be on its way.'

It was.

The following week, on my way home from the office, I went as usual to the field to see how Jenny and the foal, whom I had named Blossom, were settling in. I saw at once that something was wrong. The foal had had diarrhoea.

It was after six o'clock but, when I rang the vet, he said he would come at once, and in about half an hour he was with me.

'Have you got a shed?' he asked. 'If we can get them in, I

can give the foal an injection.'

'There's my garage, on the other side of the village,' I told him.

'Come on,' he said. 'You catch the mare, and we'll go.'

I looked at him sideways, but said nothing and, looking – I hoped – a lot braver than I felt, I climbed over the fence. Jenny immediately came at me, head down, ears back. I walked towards her, the halter in one hand, the other full of oats.

'Come along, then,' I said, hoping the vet could not see my face.

For a moment Jenny paused, uncertain whether or not to kick me back over the fence, then her nostrils caught the scent of the oats and she stopped looking like a bull about to charge, and began to walk quietly towards me. The next moment she was eating out of my hand and I had slipped the halter over her head and pulled it tight. I could hardly believe it when she did not drag me off my feet, but, instead, stood as quietly as she used to do before the foal was born. The vet lifted the wooden rail that served as a gate into the field and I led her out into the lane, the foal dancing along behind.

By now it was dark. Cars on the main road brushed close by us. A driver lowered his window and shouted something rude about not having any lights and at last we reached the garage in Trivetts Lane.

Mary, by a miracle, had chosen that evening to pay me a visit. At once she grasped the situation and opened the garage doors for us. I led Jenny inside. The foal followed and as I led the mare out again Mary quickly closed the doors again from inside, shutting herself and the vet and the filly all inside in the dark. Loud crashings and stampings followed and the high note of the foal's rather pitiful cry. Outside I hung on to the mare's halter as she rose on her hind legs, waving her huge hooves perilously near my face, and gave out a great whinny.

Eventually the doors opened and out burst the foal, the dishevelled vet and Mary.

☆ ☆ ☆

Blossom grew into a beautiful animal, taller than Jenny and finely made, showing undoubted proof of Arab blood.

I broke her to a halter but realized that I would never be able to ride her. She would need someone far more experienced and braver than I.

Jenny's temper did not improve and I never felt really happy riding her again, though I knew I must. At last I decided to sell them both. I put an advertisement in the local paper and it was not long before, with some real regret, I saw them go.

A few weeks after the sale there was a knock at my door. I opened it to find, to my surprise, Mr Foot standing there.

'I've come for the saddle and bridle,' he announced. For a moment I was nonplussed. Then I remembered that I had only had the saddle and bridle on loan and had never, in fact, paid for them. I had forgotten all about the matter.

'I've sold them,' I confessed, rather lamely.

'Sold them,' shouted Mr Foot. 'Who to?'

'I will get them back for you of course,' I said, 'or I will pay you their full value.'

'I want that saddle and bridle,' roared the farmer. 'They belonged to my sister-in-law and she wants them for her son. Who did you sell the foal to?'

Something made me begin to suspect that there might be more to Mr Foot's visit than appeared at first sight. It was not difficult to see that he had worked out that the foal would now be the right age for him to buy back at an easy price, the early stages of breeding and breaking having been done for him. I decided to keep him in ignorance.

When he saw that I was not going to tell him where the foal was he turned nasty.

'I'll have the law on you,' he shouted, 'for selling property that doesn't belong to you! I'll have you in the assizes!'

'And what about you selling a mare in foal?' I responded.

'I'll bet it's not the first time you've been in the assizes,' called Mary from the upstairs window from which she had been witnessing the proceedings. Giving us both a glare of frustrated fury, the farmer turned to go. His parting shot, as he opened the gate was:

'That foal was sired by a thoroughbred. She's worth a hundred guineas.'

9

'How would you like to work in the BBC?'

My weekend visitor was Ruth, and she and I were spread out on the grass, under the blue sky of the summer.

'I have never thought about it,' I said. 'I should hate to live in London. Think of being imprisoned in a flat, after this.' I leant up on my elbow and looked at the hills and chequered fields that surrounded the garden.

'I think you'd like it,' she said. 'It's time you thought of a change.'

I tried to put the idea out of my head. I did not really want to leave where I was but Ruth was right when she said I would have to think about a move some time, and as the days went past I found her suggestion making its presence felt ever more firmly. A few weeks later, a letter arrived from her with a notice about a job in the Corporation. I sent for particulars, and, before long – rather to my surprise – I was appointed.

Now I realized I must face the problem of moving. There was no hope of a country cottage within reach of London. All I could afford would be a couple of rooms, and the thought of no longer being able to wander into the garden in my dressing gown in the early summer morning filled me with gloom.

Suddenly I thought of Jim's boat. I remembered the first time I had been inside the boat. It was a few months after Mary had gone to live with Jim. It was January and I was riding Jenny along the towpath. There had been a light fall of snow.

'Hello,' Mary called to me from the window. I pulled Jenny up and dismounted.

It was January and I was riding Jenny
along the towpath . . .

'Come and have coffee with us this evening,' she said.

By evening the snow was falling heavily and I had some difficulty in finding my way to the towpath in the darkness. As I came down from the lane towards the wharf the canal between the snow-covered banks stretched in front of me like a black ribbon, edged with white.

I felt my way carefully to the wharf. The dark outline of the boat loomed up in front of me, framed with its coating of snow. There was a narrow plank leading from the towpath to the small aft deck. There was no handrail to grasp and I edged my way gingerly along the plank and stepped on to the deck. I heard footsteps approaching inside and a hatch was pulled back. I looked down into the softly lit cabin, in the glow of an oil lamp.

'Come in,' said Mary, opening the narrow door.

Three steps led down from the deck to the floor of the cabin below water level. Mary closed the door and slid back the hatch and bolted it, shutting out the dark night and the cold.

'Come in and sit down. Jim's just fallen in, but he won't

be long. He's changing.'

There was a locker beside the stove and Mary indicated that I should sit there, while she went to put on the coffee. I looked around. The long, narrow cabin with its barrel-shaped roof and sloping sides was like something out of a child's story book and suddenly I felt I was a child again, in a world of magic, where adventures were only round the corner. The soft light of the lamp, the slight movement of the boat and the creak of the mooring ropes were part of Treasure Island. I felt a strange tingle of excitement.

Mary came out of the galley with the coffee and in a moment Jim appeared from the far end of the boat.

'Come and see the rest of it,' he said.

Taking the Tilley lamp off its hook, he led the way along the narrow passage. Next to the living cabin, where I had been sitting, was the galley, long and narrow and fitted with a sink on one side and a large water tank beside it and on the other side, a stove, rather like a poor man's Aga. Beyond this was the bathroom, the bath on one side of the passage and the lavatory on the other. There were doors at each end which could be shut across the passage, to close the bathroom completely.

Beyond the bathroom was a sleeping cabin with a double bed and beyond this again, right in the pointed bows of the boat, was another cabin, one side of which was entirely filled by a pair of bunk beds. Here the children slept. There were lockers and built-in cupboards wherever they could be fitted, providing enough storage space for a family's belongings.

We turned round and walked back, in single file, the Tilley lamp throwing our shadows on the walls, down the length of the boat to the living cabin, where coffee was waiting.

'I built it on an old hull,' said Jim. 'It has been my home for years.'

'The canals must be restored,' he went on, 'and they will be, if enough people know and care about them. They are a wonderful way of seeing England, the unspoilt parts. They take you to places you would never find by road. The waterside inns are still much as they were when the boatmen used them, and the lock cottages and bridges were built mostly in the eighteenth century and they are worth looking at.'

He opened one of the lockers and brought out a collection of books and photographs for me to see, and as he talked, I entered further and further into this new and utterly different world.

I looked at my watch. It was nearly twelve o'clock and the world of snow and ice and solid houses of brick that never moved, came back to me.

'I must go,' I said reluctantly.

Jim pulled back the bolt on the door and slid back the hatch. The snow had stopped and a dark sky of stars filled the rectangle over our heads. I stepped up on to the deck, the cold night wind blowing on my face.

'Good night,' I called, as I felt my way along the narrow, icy plank and on to the snow-covered bank.

I looked back from the bridge to where the dark shape of the boat lay, close to the wharf. A light shone across the gleaming dark water, from the cabin where, one day, I myself would be living.

☆　　☆　　☆

I decided to have a word with Jim.

'Have you sold the boat yet?' I asked, and told him of my coming move.

He and Mary seemed pleased to think that *The Chester* might become mine and in half an hour everything was settled. I went home and began to make arrangements for the sale of my cottages, and started the search for a mooring within easy reach of London.

Little did I know how difficult it was going to be.

I began by writing to every boatyard and yachting club up and down the Thames. All proved fruitless. Then, at weekends, I went to London and tramped up and down the banks, exploring every island and inlet, with no success at all. It was the size of the boat that was against it. I was offered plenty of moorings but, as soon as I said that it was seventy feet long, the owners shook their heads. Weeks went by and I grew more and more hopeless.

At last the cottages were sold and in a few weeks I should

Struggling and heaving I managed to get three of its
legs through the window . . .

have to be out. With mixed feelings I began to pack my
belongings and to move them, a few at a time, into the boat.

The cottage became more and more bare and I looked
sadly at the emptying rooms and the garden which would
soon no longer be mine. The few years I had been there had
filled it with memories and I was leaving something of
myself behind.

Stowing my belongings and furniture on the boat was a
problem in itself. There were only two ways of getting
things on board: one was through the door, which led from
the small aft deck into the living cabin. It was only two feet
wide, so anything of any size had to go in the only other way
– through the window.

All was well until it came to the settee. I loaded it into the
back of my car, which was possible when the soft roof was
down, and drove rather carefully, since I could not see what
was behind me, down the canal bank and pulled up by the
wharf.

In the cottage it seemed to be just a normal, small-sized
settee, with the usual number of legs and arms, but when I
tried to get it through the window of the boat it suddenly
appeared to grow to an enormous size and to sprout legs
and arms at all kinds of new angles.

Struggling and heaving I managed to get three of its
legs through the window, but the fourth refused to go in. I

dragged it out again and tried another way. This time, the two legs and two arms went in, but the remaining legs struck out over the towpath, looking as if nothing would ever get them inside. I pulled it out once more and turned it upside down. That was no better; in fact, much worse. I sat on the bank to get my breath back.

I was determined it was going in. Nothing would make me take it back to the cottage again, so both of us would sit here, every now and then having another battle, until it gave in. I clenched my teeth and prepared to attack it again. Muttering my views about its ancestry, I put my shoulder underneath its back and heaved.

Suddenly, as though there had never been any difficulty, the wretched thing slid quietly through the window, landed on its four feet and arranged itself as though it had always been there.

10

At last everything was on board and the boat looked like a travelling junk store. The furniture was stacked solidly together, filling both sides of the boat so that I could only just move up and down the narrow passageway down the centre. The cottage was empty and awaiting the arrival of its new occupants in a matter of days. I had left Trivett's Lane the week before to start my work in London, but I still had no mooring for the boat. It looked as though I had bought a rather unpractical furniture store, not a home.

I was beginning to despair; then, at the eleventh hour, I was offered a mooring in a boat basin near Chiswick Bridge. It seemed the perfect place and I could not believe that my troubles were over.

Indeed they were not, but, in blissful ignorance I began to make plans for the journey to London.

The journey would have to be made in stages, at week-ends, as I had already started working at the BBC. It was almost Christmas by this time and I had to find a crew, hardy, skilful and willing for the rigours ahead.

Jim said he would start me off and promised to accompany me for as long as he could, but Mary was expecting again so he would not be able to come very far.

'I'll take the boat to Wolverhampton,' he wrote to me. 'You can join me there after Christmas and we'll go on together.'

And so it was that one frosty morning in early January I set out by car from London and headed northwards, happily ignorant of what lay in front of me.

☆　　☆　　☆

'What the blazes are you doing?' Jim's voice came through the smoke. 'Are you trying to set the boat on fire? Here, come up and take the tiller,' and he pushed past me, down the three steps from the aft deck into the living cabin, now full of smoke from end to end.

Five minutes before he had shouted to me, above the noise of the boat's engine: 'Get the fire going, will you?'

It was a bitterly cold Sunday morning in January with a raw mist lying over the deserted canal. My hands were frozen from handling icy ropes and I was only too glad to be called inside, out of the bitter air, into the shelter of the narrowboat cabin. As well as being miserably cold I was feeling utterly useless and inadequate.

Jim had started *The Chester* on her journey, as he had promised. He had left Brockley, with a friend as crew, just before Christmas. He had written to me, reporting progress, telling of frozen ropes and icy water and short, dark days. He had eventually reached Wolverhampton and here I had joined him. Together we were to take her on the next stage of the journey to London.

It had all sounded so easy when we had discussed it on a summer morning, six months before, under the heady may blossom on the canal bank at Brockley. With the optimism of the ignorant I had charged straight in and now here I was, faced with reality, in the form of seventy feet of boat and a hundred and fifty miles of canal, and too late, far too late, to back out.

I had set off early from London and after some unpleasant encounters with black ice, eventually found the outskirts of Wolverhampton. Following the map that Jim had sent me, I found my way to the ironworks where the boat was tied. There was no one about. The gaunt, empty sheds rose black and slightly unreal through the cold mist. It lay white and still above the water and gave *The Chester's* seventy foot of dark hull a kind of unreality.

I walked along the bank towards her, my feet cracking the thin ice over the rain puddles and the rime-laden grass brushing white dust on to my legs as I passed. I climbed on board, along a narrow plank from the bank, on to the small aft deck, followed by Samson, pattering close behind and investigating everything with his black nose. Jim was already on board. The hatches over the engine hole were up and he was hidden from the waist down, below the deck.

'You'd better come and watch this,' he called to me, without wasting time on greetings. 'You'll have to do it yourself in future, so you'd better know. I'm just going to start up.'

Before I had time to see what he was doing down there I felt the pulsing, reverberating throb of the sixteen horsepower engine, as the strong chug-chug-chug, which was to become so familiar a sound, broke the stillness of the morning and echoed round the deserted sheds.

Jim came up out of the engine hole, shut down the hatch cover, climbed out on to the long black roof of the boat and went forward to untie the mooring line at the bow. As she swung away from the bank, he lifted the twenty foot pole from the rooftop and ran back to the aft deck and began to sweep away the weed that had drifted against the stern of the boat, before it became entangled in the propeller.

Then, handing the pole to me, he quickly grabbed the gear lever and pushed it into 'forward', revved up the engine and leant out on the rudder. Slowly the bows of the boat came round in a half circle across the winding hole, where the canal opened into a kind of basin, wide enough for turning. The engine kept up its insistent chug-chug and now we were facing in the opposite direction and heading along the canal. The journey had begun.

All this time, except for holding the pole, I had looked helplessly and uselessly on. Jim was under the impression that he had already told me all I needed to know about managing the boat.

One morning, about a month ago, back at Brockley, he had summoned me to meet him on the boat.

'I'll just show you what you have to do,' he said as he took up the hatches over the engine.

'We'll look inside the engine first,' and with an enormous screwdriver he undid and removed the top.

'Now,' he said briskly, 'look at that.'

I looked, quite bewildered at the array of machinery and moving parts. None of it looked even remotely like anything I had ever seen before and how it all functioned I had not the least idea.

'Yes,' I said, 'I'm looking.'

'Well, now, I'll tell you what to do,' he went on: 'Open this cock first, see? And then screw down that nut. Pour some water in here. Tighten up those screws and loosen those. Put some oil in here. Undo that. Open this. Do that up. Give this a half turn to the right. Give that a quarter turn to the left. Put some grease on here. Mind you don't get any grease on there. Make sure you've got water in that. Whatever you do, don't get any water on this. Got it? It's quite easy.'

'Yes, Jim,' I replied meekly. 'I'm sure it's quite easy really.'

With hardly a pause for breath and quite oblivious of me, he continued: 'Now I'll tell you what to do when you pack up the engine for the winter. This is very important. If you get it wrong the whole thing will freeze up and split.'

'Yes, Jim,' I said again, rapidly becoming hypnotized.

'All right. Now here it is: Grease this and these and those. Open these cocks and drain this pipe. Loosen these nuts and tighten those. Undo this union. Wrap some sacking around that one. Screw down these nuts and give these two quarter turns to the right. That's all. Mind you don't forget anything.'

'No, Jim,' I said, turning my glazed eyes away from the monster that was soon to take me over. 'I'm sure I won't forget anything.'

Again, without a glance at me, which would have conveyed even to Jim that he might as well have been addressing the empty air, he went on: 'Now I'll show you how to start her. It's quite simple.'

He dropped down under the deck, amongst the machinery, unhooked from a nail a huge starting handle and fitted it, with a flourish, into the enormous flywheel. He pushed the gear lever over into neutral.

'Now,' he said, 'all you have to do is turn the handle and the engine starts. As soon as you feel it's going, bang the gear lever into 'forward'. That's all.'

He did it. A satisfying chug-chug-chug came from the engine. I came to, sufficiently, to smile admiringly.

'Now you do it,' he said.

I took the starting handle from him and almost dropped

it. After several attempts and almost standing on my head I eventually got it connected to the business end of the engine.

'Now turn it over,' said Jim, encouragingly.

I tried.

'I can't move it,' I said, desperately.

'You'll have to push harder than that,' said Jim.

'But I *am* pushing harder. It just doesn't move at all.'

'Oh well. You'll just have to find someone to do it for you.'

Now as I watched Jim navigating the boat along the winter canal with the assurance of experience and brute strength I wondered whatever I could have been thinking of to get myself into this. How could I ever have thought I could manage the boat on my own? And I was only at the beginning.

11

It was then, when I was standing idly by, watching Jim expertly handling the boat that he told me to get the fire going.

The boat had been empty for six weeks. It was damp and cold and, though now full of my furniture, it looked sad, empty and dirty, like a secondhand store. I went down the steps into the cold living cabin with its uncurtained windows. There was a small stove on the right-hand side, with a pipe leading out through the roof. It had a pair of doors in front, with little square mica windows. I had never dealt with anything like it before, but I thought it must surely be possible for me to find out what to do and so restore a little of my rapidly ebbing confidence.

I opened the doors and peered inside at the collection of cinders and ash left there from the last time it was used. There were some old newspapers and kindling sticks pushed in at the back of the stove. I screwed up some of the sheets of newspaper and dropped them in and threw a handful of sticks on top. Then I lit a match and offered it to the pile.

At once there was a loud explosion. Flames shout out of the front of the stove, burning off my front hair. A cloud of smoke belched out of the doors and filled the cabin. It swirled round and round in a grey spiral and then whooshed up the steps, out of the hatch and on to the deck. With tears streaming down my face and coughing and spluttering, I followed it.

Jim uttered a fruity curse, pushed the tiller into my hand, nearly sending me overboard, and shot down the steps into the cabin.

I looked in front of me: seventy feet of long, narrow boat, the bows so far away that they did not seem to belong, the deck below my feet vibrating with the insistent throb of the engine and slippery with the partly melted ice which had covered it.

'What do I do?' I thought, as my fingers closed round the long, smooth wooden tiller.

Jim had vanished in the smoke. I was alone.

I tried desperately to remember the little I knew about steering boats. Until that moment my experience had been limited to a quiet row on the Thames and a gentle punt down the Cherwell. Neither of these seemed to help at all at the moment. I looked at the cold, dark water ahead of me and the wintry banks on either side. There was no sign of life of any kind, no boats, no people, not even a cow in the fields.

Fortunately there was no traffic, so at least there was no one for me to run into, this still Sunday morning, as the boat headed first for the right bank and then for the left one, then sharp off to the right again, in a perfect zigzag. I was glad that Jim could not see what I was doing, though he must have felt it all.

As her nose made for the reeds and mud, first on one side and then on the other, I leant my weight, such as it was, against the tiller only just in time to bring her round before she stuck fast. I almost slipped overboard each time as the deck was so small that one step in either direction left one's foot hanging out over the water. The speed was scarcely more than a fast walking pace, but with so much boat stretching in front of me I felt I had shrunk to half the size and as though I had been left to take charge of an untamed elephant on a very small piece of string.

If only Jim would come up again from the cabin, I thought. Some of the smoke had dispersed by now but there was no sign of him. It was useless to shout. No one can hear anything above the noise of the engine on a boat like this.

In any case Jim did not seem in the least concerned. I was sure that he had no idea of what I was going through or of what might happen to the boat he had so casually put in my care. He could have no idea that I had never handled anything like it.

My ability with machinery had never been of a high order. I had only just managed to learn to drive a car. I still wondered how it had happened. I used to feel that I was the one person in the world who would never do it. The sight of the rows of buttons and switches on the dashboard and all the levers and pedals down below, not to mention the buzzing confusion of cars and lorries and pedestrians and animals all flashing past in both directions, had induced a kind of mental freeze-up. All normal reactions ceased and a slow panic began to well up from the lowest region of my stomach and spread all through until it succeeded in paralysing every limb. Heaven knows how I passed my test. And here I was, with it all happening again, only worse.

The moments dragged on. The banks seemed to flash past, while the inescapable chug of the engine hypnotized me into the same sense of utter helplessness and paralysis. And then I saw the bridge hole.

Straight ahead, a few yards in front of the bows of the boat it seemed, the canal suddenly became a narrow stream, two or three feet wide, or so it looked from where I was as it vanished into a round, dark hole, a few feet high, under the humpy bridge that took the road from one side of the canal to the other. Nothing bigger than a child's boat could get through there, there could be no doubt. And it was rushing towards me.

Nobody could get a boat under that bridge, never mind out the other side; certainly not me. Where *was* Jim?

It was no use shouting. Even if he had been interested he could not have heard me and clearly he was utterly heartless and cared nothing for me or for the boat.

The hole rushed nearer and nearer. I fixed my eyes on the far distant end of the boat and gripped the tiller even tighter. Then, as gently as I could, I moved it first one way, then the other. To my relief, the boat's nose stopped leaping from side to side and began to keep on a steady, fairly straight line. I felt a little better; was I beginning to get the hang of it? If so, it was only just in time, and the bridge was not only narrow but low. It looked at though it was going to take the roof of the boat off, followed by my head. What did one do? Duck down, so that I could not see where I was going, or stay standing up and have my head removed as we went underneath? Why, I thought yet again, had I ever embarked on this appalling venture.

I was just about to offer up my last prayer when I felt myself pushed roughly out of the way and almost overboard again. With a touch on the throttle and a skilled swing of the tiller, Jim was once more in control. I muttered something unrepeatable as I watched his practised handling, as he steered the boat gently under the bridge without event touching the sides. She glided smoothly through and out the other side.

'You'll get used to it,' he shouted. 'It's quite easy when you've done it once or twice.'

And now, I saw, we were approaching a lock. The gates at the far end were closed and the lock was full. Indicating that I was to take the tiller again, Jim put the engine into neutral and leapt ashore, as we entered the lock, to close the gates behind us. The boat moved gently forward under her own momentum, until her nose rubbed against the lower gates.

'Put her into forward gear!' yelled Jim as he leant his weight against the balance bar of the gate behind. I did what I was told and the boat, under the power of the engine, kept her bows close to the gates in front, like a dog on a lead, straining to go.

Jim was now at the lower gates preparing to open the paddles to let the water out. 'Now put her into neutral,' he shouted to me as he fitted the windlass into one of the paddles and began to wind it up.

The water began to rush through, as the lock emptied and the moving water surging forward carried the boat with it. Down, down she sank; the walls rose higher and higher on either side and once more I felt utterly alone, as Jim – on the lockside – retreated further and further from me.

'Look out!' he yelled, 'the tiller!'

I turned round, just in time to see the handle of the tiller, which had swung round in the swirl of the water, jutting at right angles over the stone paving of the lockside. In another moment it would have snapped, as the boat and I sank still deeper. Grabbing it with both hands, I swung it round, in the nick of time.

This, surely, meant I was learning fast, well on my way to becoming a reliable boat person. Jim, I thought, must have been impressed by my prompt action. He had not even seen it.

We came to rest at last, when the water level in the lock was the same as that beyond. Now the gates could be opened and when Jim had done this he stepped aboard, flicked up the throttle and took the tiller again, with no more than a casual glance to see that all the bits of boat were still there. Clearly he was utterly unaware of all I had been through in the past quarter of an hour.

Feeling quite inadequate and in the way, I went down into the galley to brew up some tea, a task I felt, at last, to be within my capabilities. I filled the pan and set it on the Primus, then went forward to the bow cabin and opened the window which looked out over the canal in front of us. Quietly the banks slid by on either side, the water parting in gentle waves as the boat moved forwards. Birds sang from the bushes on the bank. All was peace, and slowly my confidence began to return.

Suddenly I was jerked out of my reverie. The water was no longer moving and there was a strange stillness and silence. The engine had stopped. I raced back along the boat and up the steps to the aft deck. The hatch over the engine was up and Jim was down in the engine hole.

'Water pipe's split,' he called up. 'Come on down and get going on the bilge pump.'

I swung myself down beside him into the dark hole below the deck and Jim thrust the handle of the bilge pump into my hand.

'Keep it going,' he called, 'or we'll be awash.'

'Chig, chug, chig, chug,' the water spluttered through the hole in the side of the boat as I pushed the wooden handle backwards and forwards, while drips of oily water ran down my arm, and my knuckles were scraped by the rough wood of the boat's sides. Meantime, Jim repaired the pipe with rag and pieces of wire, while my spirits sank even lower as I thought to myself: 'And this is only the first day.'

12

Half an hour later the engine was going again and we chugged on down the cut with a soft rain falling. Somewhere along here we were to pick up Evelyn and Roger, who had volunteered to crew with us for a day.

It was difficult to be sure exactly where we were, in spite of the maps that we had with us. The familiar Black Country landmarks all looked different from the canal. It was a strange new world, where one saw only the underneath of roads and bridges as we ducked our heads under the network of pipes and girders and where well-known buildings and warehouses all had their backs turned.

The rain began to fall more heavily now, making a pattern of spreading ripples on the dark surface of the canal. We turned up our collars and wiped the water from our eyes. The canal was straight here, with the towpath on our left. At the far end we saw two figures, standing all alone under an umbrella and even from this distance we could see that they were very damp.

Evelyn was one of my tidier friends. Wherever you met her and whatever time of day it was, she always looked as though she had just finished dressing to go out to a special occasion.

I felt this rather badly as I never looked like that. Even when it *was* a special occasion and I had bought a new outfit it was always the same. The suit, or dress, or whatever, looked superb in the shop, hanging on the rack. Even when I tried it on in the dressing cubicle it still looked pretty special, but by the time I actually put it on to wear it something fundamental had happened to it. The seams sagged, the collar did not sit right, the skirt was far too long, or too short. It just did not fit anywhere. And it was the wrong colour, shape and design.

On top of all that it looked as though I had been wearing it for the past four days both in bed and out. It was very disheartening and people like Evelyn, who always looked ready to receive Royalty, rubbed it in continually.

Now I saw her standing on the towpath, in a mackintosh it is true, and under an umbrella, but where I would have looked like something that had, literally, been left out in the rain, she – though damp – was as crisp and pleated and pressed as if she were entirely untouched by the opened heavens.

My heart sank for her as I thought of what lay ahead, if my recent experience was anything to go by, and then it gave a kind of lamb-jump of anticipatory delight at the quite unkind thought that even she could not be proof against the worst the canal could do.

Jim steered the boat close to the bank. Roger furled the umbrella and climbed aboard and held out an arm to help Evelyn step up beside him.

They had barely had time to see where they were when Jim shouted: 'Lock coming' and they found themselves back on the towpath, each with a heavy windlass in hand.

'What's that for?' asked Evelyn, waving hers at Jim.

'You'll see. Watch what Roger does,' Jim called.

He threw the ropes ashore, forward and aft, and leapt after them to make sure they did it right and once more I was left alone with the boat to control.

With a touch on the throttle I put the engine into reverse. This did not send the boat backwards, as one might expect, but merely acted as a brake, slowing her down enough for her to enter the lock without crashing into the far gates. Feeling rather proud of my new skill I brought her straight in so that she nosed up to the far end with scarcely a judder.

'Now put her into neutral,' called Jim.

Our new crew had already been running backwards and forwards collecting up the ropes that Jim had thrown out on the bank. They pulled them in, bringing the boat gently to the lockside, and secured them around the bollards on the side of the lock.

'Now what do I do with this thing?' enquired Evelyn,

wagging her windlass at Roger as though it had somehow come into her possession by accident and she was trying to find its proper owner.

'You wind the paddles up with it.'

'What's a paddle?' she enquired. 'I thought that's what you did at the seaside, not in a canal.'

'It's the bit there in the middle of the lock gate that moves up and down,' explained Roger patiently. He rather liked Evelyn's helpless kind of questions, especially when he knew the answers.

'That's where the water goes through,' he said. 'Look, you can see them there,' and he pointed to the flat shutter-like sections in the centre of the lock gates in front of the boat.

'Come on, you two,' shouted Jim, 'get the gates closed.'

Jim went to the other end of the lock, relieving Evelyn of the windlass on the way.

'Come on,' he said, 'I'll show you how to do it.'

He fitted the windlass on to the paddle ratchet and began to turn. Slowly the paddles rose, letting the pent-up water pour through and splash in a white foam into the pound below.

'You have a go now,' he said to Evelyn. 'You've to get a good swing on it. Just imagine you're starting a 1930 car or bringing a bucket up from the well.'

Evelyn gripped the windlass with both hands.

'I can't,' she cried. 'It's stuck.'

'You'll never make a navvy that way,' said Jim, taking over and with a few easy turns bringing the paddles up to their full height.

The boat moved forward, drawn by the pull of the water, as the lock emptied. Slowly she dropped as the water drained away and the lockside – with Jim, Roger and Evelyn on it – rose higher and higher above my lonely head. The rushing sound of the water died away and swirls and eddies began to wash backwards from the gates as the levels on both sides became equal. The boat, with the engine still in neutral, began to drift back towards the upper gates.

'Look out!' yelled Jim. 'The sill.'

I looked back and there, coming up through the water, I could see the great stone step over which the gates closed. If the stern of the boat were to be caught on that and the bows continued to go down with the sinking water, the boat would 'break its back'.

'Put her into forward gear!' Jim shouted from above me. 'Keep her up, away from the gates.'

I could only just hear him against the rush of the water and the noise of the engine which sounded even louder in the bottom of the lock than out in the open, but I flicked the gear lever from 'neutral' into 'forward' and felt the engine urge the boat forward, just in time. I looked back and saw the sill rise clear of the water by about a foot and sent up a prayer of thanks to the Water Gods for their protection of the ignorant.

Jim and Roger opened the lower gates and with some triumph and much relief I steered *The Chester* out into the open pound. The crew stepped on board from the towpath and we chugged on down the empty canal.

The next lock was uphill and as we approached it the huge dark gates towered over our heads. Jim, back at the controls, steered the boat between the deep, dripping walls, black with slime. Then, handing me the rudder, he leapt from the roof of the boat up on to the lock side.

'Throw up the ropes!' he shouted, as he ran back to close the gates behind us.

Between us we coiled and cast the forward and aft ropes above our heads, to land on the lockside, and Roger and Evelyn scrambled up after them. Collecting the ropes as they went, they ran forward to open the paddles in the gates in front to fill the lock. A cascade of water poured over the bows of the boat from the pound above, rocking her from side to side. Quickly the lock filled and we rose higher and higher until we were level with the top of the lockside.

I got ready to steer out, flicking the engine into 'forward' and giving it some throttle as the top gates began to swing open. The engine note rose and the water churned in a white froth behind, but the boat remained where she was. I revved up some more, with no different result.

'There's some timber in the lock,' Jim shouted. 'It's

jamming her. Here, alongside.'

Between the boat's side and the brick lining of the lock a ten foot plank had got caught and since the lock itself was only seven foot in width, the same as the beam of the boat, it was acting as a very effective wedge, preventing the boat from moving forwards or backwards. Jim grabbed the pole from the roof of the boat and gave the plank a push to dislodge it. Then he sent it on its way out through the open gates and into the pound. From here he fished it out, and threw it on the bank.

He stepped on board and Evelyn and Roger joined him and on we went.

13

We were now approaching Birmingham. The short winter day was nearly over and it was getting dark. The canal, running under the maze of the city's streets, was black and mysterious and slightly sinister. Huge walls of factories and warehouses, patterned with dark windows, rose on either side. A network of girders and pipes crossed and re-crossed the water, low over our heads. An occasional street lamp shone over a high wall, like something in another world, and we chugged on with a strange sense of isolation.

Soon the boat entered the pitch-black mouth of a road bridge, so narrow that we could touch the sides. The roof of the boat was only a few inches from the curved brickwork overhead. Suddenly there was a horrible scraping sound. The boat came to a standstill. Jim shone a torch along the line of the roof into the darkness ahead.

'She's stuck again,' he called.

'More timber?' I shouted.

'No, it's the water level. It's too high. There's not enough space above the water for us to get through.'

'What do we do? Empty the canal with buckets?'

'No, I'll have to go back and lower the water.'

How this was to be done I had no idea. Jim jumped ashore and made off along the towpath in the direction from which we had come, while we waited, in the darkness. The level of the water, I discovered later, could be lowered by opening the paddles in the lock gates behind us. The water would then drop into the pound below and be replaced by some of the water that was now preventing us from going under the bridge.

A few minutes after Jim had gone we felt ourselves

dropping down, away from the underneath of the bridge. At last the boat swung free of the brickwork and we could see the pale light of the night sky, curving over the roof of the boat at the end of the short tunnel.

In about ten minutes Jim was back and soon we were clear of the bridge and out on an open stretch of water again.

'I think we'd better tie up,' said Jim. 'Let's call it a day.'

He steered the boat in to the bank, and switched off the engine. A strange silence followed, in which we heard the unfamiliar sound of traffic passing on the roads close by. Jim jumped ashore and fixed the mooring pins.

'Someone had better go shopping,' I said, 'if we can find the way.'

The canal here ran between high walls over which rose the dark bulk of factories and warehouses. Leaving the men to complete the mooring, Evelyn and I took a basket and set off along the towpath stepping as carefully as we could round the puddles.

At first there seemed to be no way out until, at length, we found a break in the wall, with a narrow passage-way leading away from the canal. We felt our way along it in the darkness. Suddenly there was a roar of traffic and the brilliant yellow of street lamps and we stepped out into a road. It was another world.

After the darkness and the silence and the remoteness of the canal, it hit us like a clap of thunder. It did not seem possible that two such different worlds could exist within a few yards of each other.

We walked slowly, avoiding people, and gradually and unwillingly adjusting to the noise and speed and restlessness.

As we passed a shop window I glanced sideways at the peculiar reflections. Odd people one sees in cities these days, I thought. Then I looked again, more closely, at the figure I could see there, grey with dirt and dishevelled.

It was me.

Our shopping done, Evelyn and I returned to the towpath and made our way in the darkness to where we could see the long, low black outline of the boat at her mooring. A faint but welcome light from the Tilley lamp shone from the cabin window and with a feeling of coming home we stepped on board and down into the warmth of the cabin, where a pan was boiling on the Primus, ready for tea. The men were still wet. They had not taken off their coats and anoraks, and they looked decidedly hungry.

We unpacked the basket and dropped the sausages into the frying pan, opened a large tin of beans and sliced up a loaf of bread. Supper had the particularly good taste that food has when you have worked hard for it in the open air.

Afterwards we sat talking in the lamplight for a while and then Roger and Evelyn got up to go. Jim and I stood at the cabin door and watched them disappear along the towpath until the January evening swallowed them up, leaving us strangely alone. Then Jim opened one of the lockers and took out the hammock. He hung it from two strong hooks in the cabin roof and, without undressing, swung himself into it and stretched out an arm to turn off the Tilley while I went forward to sleep in the top bunk in the far cabin.

We were expecting some more crew next day: Michael, an actor friend of mine, and Susan his wife. We had barely finished breakfast when they arrived. They were both dressed in their best town clothes, Michael in a well cut, tailored suit and Susan in a black costume and high-heeled shoes and carrying a smart handbag. Michael had the suitcases, two expensive leather ones that looked as though they were on their honeymoon.

They took one look at Jim and me in our greasy old clothes, neither of us particularly clean in our persons. Then they glanced round the boat, piled high with my belongings, covered with the dust of months and hung with spiders' webs. It was clear that it was all rather different from what they had expected. No doubt they had pictured something like a quick trip on the Thames where white flannels would be worn and the most energetic motion required of them would be the opening of a gin bottle. Jim and I discreetly withdrew, but we could hear them discussing the situation in tones of disturbed surprise. In a few moments they came up on deck.

'I think we'll go to a hotel tonight,' Michael told us.

We pulled up the mooring pins and moved off, soon entering the flight of locks behind Snow Hill Station. These six locks, which follow one after another in a continuous line, are only just wide enough to take one narrowboat at a time. *The Chester* being seven feet in beam and seventy feet long filled each lock from end to end and from side to side.

We passed through the first five locks with no problems but, as we prepared to move out of the last one, we found that it was impossible to open the single gate across the bows of the boat. In its hundred years of wear the gate had dropped on its hinges and there was no leeway because of the length of the boat.

We struggled until dark. At last Jim said: 'We'll have to get an axe and a hacksaw to it in the morning.'

As there was nothing more we could do that night, Michael and Susan, declining our invitation to supper, took their new suitcases and made off into Birmingham for a comfortable, spider-free night's rest, leaving Jim and me alone once more, imprisoned in the lock. We made fast and went to bed, hoping that there would be no boats working through before morning.

Rather to our surprise, our new crew turned up again soon after breakfast. Jim presented Michael with the hacksaw and instructed him to saw through the two inches of metal fender which protected the bows of *The Chester*, while he set to with an axe.

A couple of hours and several blisters later the men at last edged the heavy gate across the bows of the boat and she was free. We moved out into the British Waterways Basin, tied up and made ready to leave her there until the following weekend. Our journey that day had been about two hundred yards.

We unloaded our gear, shut down the hatch and locked up, as well as one can lock a boat, and made our way across the wharf to the gate. It was padlocked and barred. We had forgotten that it was Sunday morning.

The walls surrounding the basin were six feet high and topped with spikes. There seemed to be no other way out. In one corner was a heap of old packing cases. Jim and

Michael dragged them to the wall and piled them one on top of each other.

'Come on!' cried Jim, giving me a heave up on to the rickety heap.

'What about Samson?' I said, as I rocked about on the top. 'He'll never get over.'

'Oh yes, he will,' said Jim, grabbing the dog by the neck and tail, all seventy pounds of him. For a moment the two of them rocked backwards and forwards on the swaying packing cases, then, with a plump, Jim dropped him over the wall into the street below. The rest of us followed, landing in various undignified positions on the far side of the wall. Michael and Susan, looking considerably less *soigné* than when they arrived, picked up their elegant suitcases while Jim and I hoisted our raggy bundles on to our shoulders. We thanked them for their labours and went our separate ways.

The plan was that the boat should be moved at the weekends, as I was now working at the BBC. By the following Friday the roads were so bad that I delayed my journey from London until Saturday morning. I set off early and quickly found that the roads were covered with black ice.

I reached the highest point of the route, on the top of the Chilterns, a few minutes before eight o'clock. Suddenly I felt the car go out of control. The steering wheel whipped round in my hands and I spun round with it. The next moment I found myself facing back the way I had come. Fortunately the car was still on its wheels and, equally fortunately, the road was empty. I sat there in the winter morning dusk until some of my courage returned. Then I edged out across the road in bottom gear and set off once more in the direction of Birmingham.

It began to snow as I approached the city. It was bitterly cold and overcast with heavy dark clouds. I found my way to the wharf where we had left the boat. Jim was already there, looking intensely busy, as he always seemed to do. He started the engine and we were ready to move. We were untying the ropes from the bollards when we heard a hail from the wharfside.

'Do you want any crew?'

Jane, in yellow windcheater and jeans, came alongside. She put her hand on the boat's side with a familiar, even affectionate touch.

'I heard you were going to London,' she said. 'Can you do with a crew – two of us? I can knit and steer at the same time.'

'Come aboard,' I called. 'You're welcome. You can take the tiller straightaway.'

I looked around for her friend and was surprised when she revved up the engine and headed the boat out of the basin without him (or her). She must have known what I was thinking for, in a moment, she shouted: 'My friend is on his way. He should be along any moment.'

It all seemed odd to me, but I was becoming less and less surprised at everything that happened on the canal.

In a moment we rounded a bend and came upon a pair of working boats, heading towards us. Jane hailed them and they drew alongside, close enough for us to see the paintings on the insides of the cabin doors: the traditional roses and castles, and the shining brass rings round the little chimney on top of the cabin. A group of dark-headed, dark-eyed children stared at us out of the doorway.

There was a passenger on the butty. He stepped across on to the little aft deck of *The Chester*.

'This is Peter,' Jane shouted to us.

Any other introductions were drowned by the sound of both engines, but it did not seem to matter. The working boats swung away and chugged on towards Birmingham, the children still watching us. What a strange life for them, I thought, their contacts with anyone besides their parents so brief and infrequent. Few of them had more than an odd day or two's schooling, while the family boat was unloading at Brentford Docks, then off again. They were, indeed, water gypsies.

Jane and Peter at once took over the navigation, with the skill of old hands. I set about making pots of tea, marvelling at the timing of the operation and much relieved to have the boat in hands other than my own. Soon, mugs were being passed up to the deck and, for the first time since the journey started, I began to enjoy the experience. I collected the empty mugs from the cabin top, washed them up and hung them back on their hooks in the galley. Then I went forward to the bow cabin where, leaning out of the open window of the boat, I could watch the bows cut their way through the quiet water.

Moorhens scuttled across in front, coots jerked their way from side to side of the canal and a kingfisher flashed its brilliant blue and disappeared into the bank. A mile further on, a heron rose from his silent sentry post and flapped his slow way in front of us. A few yards ahead he dropped into the reeds and waited, standing motionless, until we came up with him. Then he rose, lifting his dropping legs as though he had almost forgotten them, flew in front again and, once more, dropped down among the reeds. For more than a mile he led the way, always waiting until we came up with him and then, lifting himself with trailing legs and long, loose wings, he flew ahead of us. At last, rounding a bend, we came upon a second bird. Our heron dropped in beside it and there we left them, standing side by side, watching us as we chugged on through the countryside.

Evening came on. We had planned to tie up at a lock about five miles south of Birmingham but we were still some distance away when the darkness of the January evening began to fall. As the light faded I stood at the window of the bow cabin, watching the lines of ripples spreading away on either side. There was no sound except the chug of the engine to break the stillness.

Suddenly the dream was broken. The ripples had ceased. We were no longer moving. I turned back along the boat's length, and up on to the deck. The boat lay at an angle across the canal, her bows wedged in a bed of reeds, the propeller churning uselessly.

'We're on the mud,' Jim called out.

He climbed on to the cabin roof and picked up the twenty foot pole which was always there, at the ready. He carried it along to the bow end and tried to push her off, but her nose was well buried in the reeds and the wind, blowing quite hard now across the canal, was driving her further in.

'We'll have to try the anchor,' Jim shouted.

Together we dragged the three foot long anchor from where it had been stowed for the journey in the forward cabin and hauled it up on to the aft deck. Jim lifted it and cast it behind us as far as he could. It disappeared with a splash into the dark water and we started to haul. Our hands slipped along the wet rope and for a moment it seemed as though we were moving. Then there was a sudden jerk and the anchor broke the surface of the water. We hauled it on to the deck again on its dripping rope and wondered what to do next.

It was quite dark by now, and we watched anxiously for approaching boats. We had no lights, and any other boat would be unable to see us until it was too late to avoid a collision.

'Someone'll have to go ashore,' said Jim.

'I'll go,' said Peter.

Jim handed him a torch and the end of a rope and let him down a narrow plank over the bows. We all watched anxiously to see how far he would sink into the cold water. He at last touched the muddy bottom.

'OK,' he shouted. 'Come on, Jane, climb over my back.'

Jane hesitated for a moment, looking at him standing thigh deep in water. Then she crouched down, put a foot on his bent back and hurled herself over him into the reeds. We saw them pick themselves up and scramble out of the water up on to the bank beyond. Then we watched the bobbing light of their torch as they vanished in the dark, leaving Jim and me alone on the deck, the boat still lying at an angle, blocking the canal and the wind and rain lashing our faces.

Still hoping there would be no other boats moving that night, we waited; five minutes, ten minutes, a quarter of an hour, with no sound but the slash of the rain and the wild buffeting of the wind, against the constant background of the throbbing engine.

At last, from behind us, on the opposite bank, we heard a shout. Jim coiled a rope.

'Coming over,' he yelled into the wind to the invisible voice.

The rope snaked through the darkness and fell on the towpath beside Peter and Jane.

'Pull hard astern!' Jim shouted as he put the engine into reverse and opened the throttle. The rope tautened, the propeller flayed the water, a shudder passed through the boat, but she stayed exactly where she was.

'Take a turn around a tree, and throw the line back to us,' Jim yelled through the wind. We took up the slack and leant our weight against it as hard as we could, the engine still going astern.

Nothing happened. It seemed as though the wind, beating against us, and now almost a gale, was too strong. We leaned harder on the rope, the rain lashing across our faces and half blinding us. Just as we felt there was no more that we could do we felt a very slight easing on the rope. We pulled in the inch or two of slack and hauled again.

She was moving!

Inch by slow inch she slipped from the sucking hold of the mud and at last we felt her afloat again beneath our feet. Jim put the engine in forward gear and drew in to the bank. Jane and Peter, thoroughly soaked, their hair flattened to their heads with the rain, climbed aboard again.

14

There was still a pair of locks to work through before we could reach our mooring place. Keeping a straight course against the gale was almost impossible. Jim did his best to hold the boat's bows in line with the entrance to the lock but the canal widened here into a kind of basin just in front of the lock. In the blackness and driving rain it was almost impossible to see the opening ahead and he missed. The wind blew us across the water and into the bank.

'She's stuck,' Jim called. 'We're on the mud again.'

I felt I had heard that before. 'Now what?' I thought.

'Come on,' called Jim, 'we'll have to rock her off. Everyone up on deck!'

The rain was now a deluge and shouts of command and suggestions were carried away on the wind, but all four of us gathered together on the few square feet of deck, slippery with the wet, and began to swing our weight from side to side. Our feet slipped on the wet canvas, but we held on as well as we could to anything firm within reach, while the drenching rain ran in streams down our necks.

Nothing happened.

Silent and numb with cold, we went on swinging from foot to foot for what seemed hours. At last Jim shouted to me: 'You'd better empty the bilges.'

Up went the hatch covers and down I climbed into the pitch-dark engine hole. I could not see where the pump was, but feeling my way along the boat's oaken side, I eventually found the handle and started the engine. Swinging it to and fro I pumped, but as fast as I pumped the water out the torrential rain filled up the bilges again through the open hatch.

In the meantime, Peter had been on a reconnaissance tour. Now we heard him climbing back on board.

'There's a working boat tied up over there by the lock,' he announced. 'I'll go and ask them to help us.'

He jumped ashore and made off in the direction of the lock. He had not gone far before we heard a splash, and peering through the murk, we saw him scrambling out of the water and up on to the bank; but he had been so wet before that the ducking made little difference.

In a few moments two large men, led by Peter, appeared on the bank beside us. A mighty push by the three of them sent the boat well out into the main channel again. Jim revved up the engine and steered out once more towards the narrow entrance of the lock.

This time we made it and, once inside the lock, we were sheltered from the worst of the gale. We worked through into the second lock and decided that we would tie up there in the bottom for the night. Jim and Peter made fast the mooring lines round the bollards while Jane and I got the Primus going for drinks.

An hour after we had first entered the basin we were at last inside, down in the cabin, warming our stiff hands round mugs of tea and nursing baked potatoes in their jackets that had been cooking in the oven for the past four hours. Peter swallowed his tea in a few gulps.

'Come on,' he said to Jane. 'Time we were gone.'

'OK,' Jane replied. 'I'm ready.'

Then to us: 'Thanks for the trip.'

'Thanks to you,' I said. 'We couldn't have done it without you.'

'See you somewhere on the cut one day,' said Jane and, still grasping their hot potatoes, she and Peter climbed out on to the deck and up on to the lockside. The last we saw of them they had reached the towpath, where they were immediately lost in the wild night. When they had gone I realized that we did not even know their second names.

As they vanished into the dark I suddenly remembered that Samson had not been ashore for hours.

'What shall we do?' I asked Jim despairingly. 'He will never get up on the lockside.'

'Oh yes, he will,' said Jim and he grabbed Samson, as

before, by the tail and neck.

'Up you go!' he called.

He lifted him bodily, shoulder high and pushed him on to the top of the lock. A quick round of the bollards and he was back inside with us.

At last, damp and aching, we were just about to turn in, when we heard a voice hailing us from the lockside above us. It was the lock keeper.

'Hi!' he shouted. 'I shouldn't stay there if I was you. The lock gates leak. You'll be on the mud by morning and there'll be working boats coming through early.'

I felt that nothing more could possibly happen as we climbed out in the dark, blustering rain once more. We untied the ropes and opened the lock gates, ready to take the boat out to a fresh mooring place.

Then I realized that I was on the wrong side of the lock. The boat and Jim were both on the other side and there was a gap of dark water lying between, and ever widening as the boat drifted towards the open gates. The way back, to join Jim, lay across the top of the lock gates behind the boat. Barely nine inches wide, the wood was slippery with the icy rain. There was a ten foot drop into the cold, dark water on the far side.

Paralysed with fright, I thought: 'I can't do it. Nothing can make me walk across those gates in this tempest.'

I stood shivering, alone in the howling dark. Jim, as usual, was utterly unaware of what was happening. He probably did not even know where I was. It would have been useless to shout for help and even I had my pride. There was really no choice and, clenching my teeth to stop them chattering with cold and fright, I grasped the low rail that ran across the top of the gates with both my frozen hands. Then, inch by inch, I crept across, shuffling my feet sideways and not daring to look down into the roaring, swirling water below.

The crossing seemed endless. I felt as though I had never been anywhere in my life but on the narrow icy top of a lock gate in a howling storm. Hours later, as it seemed, I reached the other side and with wordless gratitude I felt firm ground beneath my feet again. But I was not home yet.

The boat was still in the lock, six feet below me. It was

obvious that I had to jump, but on to what? The roof was curved and wet and slippery and if I slipped I should go down between the boat and the lockside. Jim was already on board. He seemed to have forgotten that I had ever been there.

In the dark and howling wind it all seemed incredibly dangerous, with the boat swinging backwards and forwards across the lock. I felt utterly alone. Then I saw Jim's head coming up out of the cabin. He looked round vaguely, as though something was missing.

'Jim!' I cried. 'I'm here!'

He looked up and seemed to recognize me.

'Jim! I'm coming down! Catch me!'

Closing my eyes I flung myself recklessly out into space. I landed in his arms, very nearly taking us both off the slippery roof into the water. He disentangled me and stood me on my feet.

'Why didn't you wait until I'd taken her out of the lock, you nut?' he said.

We were close enough to touch the lock walls if we leant over far enough towards one side and, hand over hand, we edged the boat out from the sheltering lock into the open pound. Jim jumped ashore with the bow line and a mooring pin and handed the stern line to me. We tied her firmly fore and aft and stumbled back, wet and speechless, into the cabin. The wind was still lashing the trees and whipping up the water when, aching, exhausted and fully clothed, we crawled into our sleeping places, I in the bunk and Jim in the hammock.

Not even the roar of the wind and the pounding of the boat against the bank could keep us awake.

Morning came, still and calm. A robin sang from the bushes on the bank. Not a ripple stirrd the mirrorlike surface of the water and in the pale, clear light of day, the night's storm seemed as though it had never been. I looked back at the lock gates and wondered that I could ever have been so terrified.

Jim got the engine started and we set off in the gentle

Morning came, still and calm. I looked at the lock gates
and wondered that I could ever have been
so terrified . . .

A robin sang from the bushes on the bank . . .

sunshine down the long pound. On this quiet winter Sunday there were no boats moving. We had the canal to ourselves and as the green banks slid by, with nothing in sight but grazing cattle and an occasional moorhen wig-wagging its way across the water, I found myself drifting into a strange new world of peace and solitude, where time no longer counted.

This, I thought, was the way to see England; England as she was before the endless traffic made roads hideous; when roads themselves linked communities instead of bypassing them, on a scale that reduced individuals to insignificance. Here, on the waterways, there is time to stare, to watch, to listen; nobody is weaving a mad race to arrive five minutes earlier at a place one does not really want to go to, but is happy to drift on in a timeless contentment. I thought of what Jim had said about the miles of waterways, mainly unspoilt and hardly found, waiting for people to use and enjoy them.

The grey stone bridges passed, one by one, occasionally with a group of Sunday strollers leaning over the top, who watched us with interest. It was unusual at that time to see any traffic on the water, apart from the occasional pair of working boats.

The strollers must have wondered what we were doing. We hardly fitted into the usual category of pleasure boats, travelling as we were in mid January, and *The Chester*, in much need of a coat of paint, did not look like a holiday cruiser.

Small boys, and men also, kept pace with us along the towpath, often arriving at the next lock ahead of us. They opened the gates and leant over, ready to catch our mooring lines and hold them while we worked through.

The morning passed without incident. I took turns with Jim at the tiller and we ate our lunch of hunks of bread and cheese as we went along. And now we were approaching a tunnel. In front of us the canal seemed to disappear into the darkness of the hill, through a very small opening.

We chugged on towards the entrance. As we approached, the hole grew larger and larger until at last it drew us in to its darkness. For a moment all was black. The cold, dank air closed round us, making us shiver. We turned up our coat collars. Then, far ahead of us, appeared a pinpoint of light. We chugged on in the blackness.

Water poured down our necks from the tunnel roof and the insistent throb of the engine, magnified in the confined space, reverberated against the narrow walls, drowning our voices. Slowly we approached the light at the far end, now grown to a circle the size of a silver sixpence. Moment by moment the circle grew larger, until it appeared like a bright moon at the end of the dark passage. As we drew nearer we could see the perfect reflection of the tunnel roof in the still water, so that it seemed that we were travelling in a beautifully rounded cylinder, half filled with transparent water.

Little by little the circle spread its circumference outwards. The light grew brighter and brighter and now we could see trees and bushes overhanging the banks beyond the tunnel. The bows of the boat broke through the stillness of the water and the reflection was gone. In a moment we were out in the pale winter sunshine, in a world of brilliant light, as though newly painted.

The contrast quickly faded. The greens and muted greys and browns returned to their accustomed colours. The sound of the engine died to a quiet throb once more and we were able to hear the birds singing.

Before dark we had reached our mooring place above the Hatton Flight, beside the top lock. Here Jim had left his motor cycle which was to take us both back to the City. The sun had gone and the January evening was cold. We stepped from the boat into a bitter winter air and in the growing darkness we made fast the mooring lines.

Jim started the motor cycle, the violent sound ripping the silence, and told me to climb on the pillion. I buried my head in his back, stretched my arms as far round him as they would go and closed my eyes. In a moment we were in the middle of the roar of traffic on the main road, heading back to Birmingham. Half an hour later, stiff and aching, I stumbled off the back, thankful that the journey was over.

This was Jim's last journey with me; Mary was pregnant again. Now I had to find a crew to help me to bring the boat the remaining sixty miles to London.

15

'Geoffrey, do you know anyone who'd like to crew a narrowboat down the canal from Warwick to London?'

Geoffrey was in the River Police, as well as being my bank manager and a very old friend.

'Well, yes, I think so,' he said. 'I would.'

I hung up the phone, wondering if I ought to have warned him about what he was in for; that it was not like a gentle cruise along the Thames, that it was still January and that there could be ice on the canal, that the boat was cold, hung with cobwebs and liable to stop moving, miles from anywhere, without any warning. Before I had come to a decision, the phone rang. It was Geoffrey.

'Can Madeleine come too?'

'Well, yes, of course,' I said haltingly.

It was bad enough to lead Geoffrey into goodness knows what troubles, but how would his wife take to life on board *The Chester*?

'Ah, well, they'll soon find out,' I thought, discarding all responsibility.

Five minutes later the phone rang again.

'The boys would like to come too, if that's all right. And Aurea.'

'Yes. Yes, of course. They can all come.'

The boys were, in fact, young men and, like their father and mother, they were over six feet tall. Christopher, the elder, was training to be an architect and Hugh was still thinking of what particular way the world was going to benefit from his skills, which lay mainly – and fortunately for me – in messing about with machinery. Both of them took after their father, who was a wizard with tools. He built

106

the first house that he and Madeleine lived in and half built all their succeeding ones. Aurea was just fourteen and would soon be up amongst the six-footer family. With my five feet and half an inch I found that my view of the world was very different from theirs.

I drove up to Warwick on the Saturday following and slept on the boat at the mooring above the Hatton flight where Jim and I had left her the weekend before.

On Sunday morning I slept late and awoke to pouring rain. I had only just cleared away the breakfast when I saw my new crew trudging along the towpath, well disguised in oilskins and sou'westers.

'Michael and Susan ought to see this,' I thought. 'These are professionals.'

They climbed aboard and suddenly the boat seemed full. I crept about under their arms and provided them with mugs of coffee. No time was wasted sitting down and talking and within half an hour they had the engine started, the mooring pins up, ropes coiled and were chugging in the direction of the top lock of the Hatton flight.

The flight consisted of twenty-one locks leading downhill, opening one out of another. As we approached the first we could see the giant staircase striding down the hillside, flanked by the double line of white posts and the heavy, black balance bars of the gates; and as we dropped down, through lock after lock, the wet timbers gleamed chestnut and green and yellow above us.

There was no stopping once we had started. Any boats coming up the flight would have to wait until we had reached the bottom, since there was no passing room in the locks.

It took my novice crew three hours of non-stop toil all through that wet Sunday morning, but by the time we reached the bottom we were aching and soaking and considerably more skilful at winding paddles and opening and closing gates than we had been at the top. As we chugged out of that last lock I looked back at the huge timbers and the black walls, stretching back up the hill like the steps of a giant's castle and felt we had had a good day.

It was afternoon and though the rain had stopped it had

already begun to grow dusk. The wise plan, I thought, would be to tie up, but the men were all for pressing on.

We had gone no more than a few hundred yards when the engine stopped with a splutter. We pulled in to the bank and tied up and the men took up the engine hatch to see what was wrong.

As they lifted the hatch a cloud of steam rose from the engine. It looked very hot. Most of what Jim had told me about the engine had gone in at one ear and out at the other, but what I had understood and remembered was that it must be kept cool. For this to happen there had to be a stream of water coming out of the hole at the side of the boat.

I looked over to where it ought to be. Nothing. Anxiously remembering what happens to a car engine when it runs out of water, I leant further over, hoping I'd missed it somehow. But no; not a drop of water was coming out of the hole. I began to feel hot too, thinking of the cost of a new engine.

Hugh swung himself down into the engine hole and began to unscrew the top of the diesel. Out came the bits, one at a time, until, in a few minutes, the deck was strewn with unidentifiable pieces of machinery.

'I hope you know how to put them all back, dear Hugh,' I thought to myself. An hour passed. There was nothing to show but an array of spanners and engine parts and darkness was falling.

'No good,' said Hugh. 'I don't know what's wrong.'

'Well, we can't leave her here,' said Geoffrey. 'We'd better get back near the lock keeper's cottage. We'll have to leave her there until next weekend.'

The engine being in pieces, the only way to move the boat now was to haul her on ropes. Geoffrey gave her a mighty push off the bank with the twenty foot pole, but she did not move. Once more, she was well and truly on the mud. By now it was quite dark, and it was clear that we would never get her back up to the cottage.

'We'll have to tie her somewhere here,' said Geoffrey.

'What to?' asked Christopher.

There was not a tree in sight, not even a bush. A broad bed of rushes and shallow muddy water lay between us and the bank. There was no firm ground where the mooring pins could be driven. There was nothing in sight but a telegraph pole, in the field beyond.

'That'll have to do,' said Geoffrey, happily ignoring the possible reactions of the Post Office.

'And how are *we* to get off?' asked Madeleine. 'We're not all as agile as you, you know.'

'And what about Samson?' I added.

'You can climb along the ladder,' said Hugh. 'If you do fall in, you won't drown anyway.'

The ladder had been lying along the roof of the boat, since the beginning of the journey. It was really just part of my furniture and apart from tripping over it every time I walked along the roof I had not given it a thought. Now we hauled it down and laid it from the aft deck, across to the bank.

Our gear was packed up ready, seaboots, bedding, tools and milk bottles. Christopher went over first and when he was safely on the bank we threw everything over to him. Then the rest of us followed, some walking upright, some crawling unashamedly on all fours. Samson ran backwards and forwards along the roof, barking madly, until at last we persuaded him to jump across the gap.

We tied the bow rope round the telegraph pole and, by going well into the field, found a firm piece of ground to drive in a mooring pin to take the stern line. Hugh and Christopher pushed the ladder back on to the boat then, in the darkness, we gathered up our belongings and strung them round our necks and began to make our way across the ploughed field to the road.

That night, we discovered later, the boat broke loose; the following morning the lock keeper found her adrift, across the canal. He rescued her and brought her up to his cottage and tied her securely until we returned the following weekend.

When I reached home I rang Jim and reported the disaster.

'Do you think we've wrecked the engine?' I asked.

'Can't tell. You could have. I expect you've done

something silly. I'd better come down and have a look at it.'

The following Saturday morning Jim arrived early. He took up the hatch cover and let himself down into the engine hole. I prepared myself for the worst.

Ten minutes later he emerged.

'The engine's all right,' he said. 'It's the water pump. It hadn't any water in it. I suppose you didn't think of priming it?'

We were now into February.

A heavy fall of snow was followed by days of subzero temperatures and the canal froze from side to side. All traffic on the water stopped. The working boats tied wherever they could, imprisoned with their cargoes, until a thaw came to set them moving again.

Here, on the water, traffic is still dominated by changes of season and temperature and is helpless until the weather changes. It takes a great deal more to bring road and rail traffic to a stop and it is not surprising that the impatience of manufacturers, drivers and consumers has almost put an end to canal transport. Perhaps, with the end of fuels in sight, the canals may come back into use, if it is not too late by then. We have not only allowed them to silt up and fall into decay, but the restless spirit of the time seems to threaten more than the existence of a canal system in itself. In our ruthless destruction of the countryside with concrete, and webs of soulless roads, out of scale with man, we are very close indeed to annihilating everything in England that has the power to feed the spirit.

The Chester was imprisoned, along with every other boat in the Midlands, while the ice thickened daily across the water. Each morning the lock keeper broke the ice round her and adjusted the mooring lines, to keep her from being broken by the pressure. At the weekend we went to see how she was.

As we crunched along the snow covered towpath her

black hull looked larger than ever against the white landscape, capped with a smooth covering of untouched snow along the cabin roof.

We opened up and got the fires going and a kettle on to boil. Then Hugh and Christopher swept the snow off the roof and scraped the ice from the windows. In a short time we were all warming our hands round hot mugs of tea and looking out from the warmth of the cabin at the white world and the snow-laden trees.

When we were well thawed out the men took up the hatches to turn the engine over and I prepared to pump the bilges.

This messy job had to be done regularly, at least once a fortnight. The first thing was to prime the pump, as Jim had so carefully pointed out. This was done by pouring several pints of water into the top of the pump. The water had to be drawn up from the canal by lowering a tin over the side on a piece of string, without, if possible, letting it go.

I lowered the tin through a gap in the broken ice, holding the string as well as I could, then drew it up over the side, trying not to slop the freezing oily water all over myself, then down I went into the engine hole.

The pump was immediately below the deck in such a position that it was impossible to tip the tin up enough to pour the water into the top. I took out the metal stopper from the top of the pump and tipped the tin up as far as it would go. About a quarter of its slimy contents found its way into the pump. The rest went over me.

Now I needed at least three hands: one to put the stopper back, another to screw it down and a third to start pumping, before the water ran right through, never mind disposing of the empty tin. Unless all these operations were done at speed the water was all gone and I had to start all over again. Every tinful of water removed so carefully for this purpose from the canal only helped to fill the bilge even fuller and make the job more urgent.

In time I learned to be cunning and to line up a series of tinfuls of water in readiness, but whatever one did it never ceased to be a wet and messy business. Later, when I was living in the boat, I used to invite a series of male visitors, carefully spacing their visits to coincide with bilge-pumping days, but even this was not successful. When they arrived, dressed in their best suits, I had not the heart to say anything about bilges. I waited until they had gone and then did it myself.

On this occasion I primed the pump until the engine floor was awash, but without success. The satisfactory feeling of a working pump, clob-clobbing with a strong movement, never came. I called for Hugh.

With a huge spanner he took the pump to pieces. The metal parts inside were cracked right through – the work of the frost. As well as this he found that the fuel pipe was leaking. It all seemed horribly disastrous, especially on a Sunday afternoon. We were going to need a blacksmith to mend them for us and where could he be found?

When everybody had had a good look at the useless bits of machinery we packed up, closed down the hatch and trudged back to the car. Then we hopefully set off into the nearest town, in search of help. Much to my surprise, we found a mechanic in a garage who seemed to know all about the problem. He promised to have the repairs ready for us by the following weekend.

16

The boat was frozen in for six weeks. During all this time the lock keeper looked after it. Every day he went over the mooring lines and adjusted them and each morning he broke the ice around her.

'Just imagine your garage man looking after a car you left parked on his forecourt, like that, without being asked,' said Geoffrey. 'And not expecting a tip either.'

The canals, and the workers on them, belong to an age that is gone, when the speed of a waterborne boat or a good horse was the fastest means of transport, and when life left time for courtesy and neighbourliness. Something of this old tranquility lingers along the waterways and the people of the canals still live a little apart from the world as it is today. If you are in difficulties they will come to your aid. We were often pulled off the mud by passing boats. The boatmen did not grudge the time they gave and time, for them, was important.

We never passed their boats without getting a nod of greeting and the children, who spent their lives in the little cabins, six feet square, waved shyly as they passed.

It is impossible to lock a boat so that no one can get in and out and, for five months, *The Chester* was tied, unattended during the week, with all that I possessed on board. Nothing was taken, in all that time, except a set of horse brasses and a length of cheap curtain material.

☆   ☆   ☆

At last the thaw came and we went up for the last time to where the boat had lain imprisoned for six weeks. My mother, who thinks of these things, had given me a small present to give to the lock keeper for his wife, as a slight return for his kindness and care. When we arrived he came out from his lockside cottage to greet us and I gave the present to him. We all trooped down the towpath and climbed on board *The Chester*.

We has just opened up and I had got the kettle going when I saw the lock keeper's wife coming down the towpath towards the boat.

'Won't you come on board?' I asked. 'It's a bit untidy but the kettle's just about to boil and I can give you a cup of tea.'

'No,' she said. 'I can't stop. I just came to thank you for the present.' Then she hesitated, put her hand up to her mouth and said:

'I'm sorry to be like this. I've got no teeth in. I've just had 'em all out. I was all right,' she added, 'till I had the pioneer.'

My mother always believes that the moment I am out of her sight I will be robbed, violated or have my throat cut. When she discovered that I intended to live alone on the boat her imagination ran riot. As I waved goodbye each Friday night on my way to the canal she gave me all her usual good advice:

'Drive carefully, dear and remember to lock your door at night' (something I frequently forgot to do). 'Do put your valuables away safely.' (I could never find out what my valuables were). But now she was able to add a whole lot more:

'Make sure the hatch is firmly shut before you go to bed. Do be careful going across the lock gates,' and, her favourite one: 'Do make sure you tie the boat near other people, dear.'

I thought it was kinder not to tell her that this was usually quite impossible.

Perhaps she had some justification for her anxieties, considering the spots I had been in, once or twice in the past. There was for instance, the time when Mary and I

114

went camping in Yorkshire. It was a warm August Friday and we were looking forward to a peaceful couple of days in the country after a particularly gruelling week trailing students in Lancashire mill town schools.

We picked up a young friend, Alice, from her home in Hebden Bridge and then began to climb the hill on to the moors over to Keighley, but the climb must have been too much for my aged car. About a mile out of Skipton, we heard an ominous rattle. It was no good hoping that it was something caught in the wheel. It was the big end. This, however, was nothing to what was to follow.

Fortunately the rattle had made itself heard just outside the Craven Heifer. The landlord kindly allowed us to use his telephone to arrange for a tow back to Skipton and to leave our camping gear in the bar while we reconnoitred for a place to put up the tent for the night.

We found a friendly farmer's wife, who gave us a Yorkshire welcome and said of course we could camp on the farm. She came to the door and pointed: 'Over there, in that field, on t'other side o't beck,' she said.

We nodded to her and to each other and thanked her and moved off in the direction she had pointed. Each of us felt sure that the others knew where she meant. It was a grave mistake.

The spot we chose was idyllic, a patch of soft green turf beside a clear babbling brook. We set up the tent, unpacked the frying pan and cooked sausages and bacon, and then lay back on the grass and gazed at the stars in deep content-ment; a prelude to disaster.

The first trouble was the midges. It seems that they never go to bed. All night, for them, is breakfast time, and we were the breakfast.

By five in the morning we could stand no more. We crawled out of the tent on to the dewy grass and lit two fires, making them as smoky as possible, which was not difficult since this is the general state of most of our camp fires. Then lying in the line of smoke, we choked and spluttered ourselves to sleep again, kippered but unbitten.

Two hours later we stirred. There was something or somebody outside the tent. Something with large feet and heavy breath. It also had a chain. We closed the tent door, without looking out and prayed that it – or he, as it obviously was – would go away.

But no. The breathing came closer. The large feet hit the tent pegs, making the whole tent shake and judder. Alice, who is frightened of anything larger than a hen, got behind Mary.

'What is it?' she whispered.

There was another loud clatter as our visitor put his feet in the pile of unwashed tin plates and frying pans; then a crash as the milk cans went over. By now the identity of the stroller was fairly clear and, knowing from experience how much cows and their male relatives enjoy eating oilskin, we dragged in all the edges of the groundsheet that were protruding from under the tent. Then we huddled together, waiting for the end.

When the plates were all licked clean the bull applied himself to the tent itself. Up and down, up and down, his tongue made a thorough job of cleaning the outside. The little tent, none too secure at any time, rocked and swayed under his pressure and we watched, in fascinated horror, the movements of the canvas as his nose passed up and down.

He came a step nearer. We shuffled further back into the tent, but the space, six feet by four, did not give us much room to get away. From corner to corner we moved, Alice and I well behind Mary, who was both bigger and braver than us.

Alice was cold with fright. At last she could bear it no longer.

'I'm going,' she said.

We tried to stop her.

'Better to die together than in ones and twos,' we said, but it was no use. She opened the end of the tent that was farthest from the bull, crawled out on hands and knees and raced across the field.

We thought it would be the last we should see of her, expecting to hear the bull charging across the field after her, but nothing happened. No sound came from Alice and our visitor continued his shampooing of the tent as before.

We later found that Alice had reached the other side of the boundary wall with nothing worse than muddy pyjama legs and thistle-torn feet.

Mary and I, alone in the tent, felt we could rely on Alice to organize a rescue party and we waited, hopefully if fearfully, our sympathies for explorers of all kinds increasing every moment. However, nothing happened. Instead of going for help, Alice just sat there, in her pyjamas, watching our approaching end.

Meanwhile, back in the tent, Mary and I clutched each other more closely. The bull's attacks were now becoming more concentrated as he pressed his great head against the tent pole, which swayed from side to side under the weight, carrying the tent with it. Mary grasped the pole with both hands and tried with all her strength to keep it upright. Suddenly there was a snap and the canvas fell in folds over the broken pole and us.

Mary let go and we retreated as fast as we could to the other end of the tent, pushing our way underneath as though we were taking part in some ghastly obstacle race. We crouched close to the remaining pole, the tent draped round our shoulders like an unwieldy cloak.

We were now at the bull's mercy. In a moment we should see his horns coming under the canvas and he would lift the little tent off the ground and us with it and toss us lightly into the beck, or, if he did not find that interesting enough, he would trample us to death beneath the canvas, well mixed with bedding, margarine and the Primus stove.

Our only hope was to follow Alice's cowardly example and make a dash for it out of the back door, only now there would be nothing to take the bull's mind off us as we made our bid for freedom; and time was running out.

The wall was a long way away and we felt sure that the bull could run faster than us, in bare feet and nightdresses. The beck, on the other hand, was close by. To be on the other side of it would put water between us and him and perhaps, with four feet to control, he might, we hoped, stumble among the stones. In any case this was no time to deliberate. Mary cautiously opened the end of the tent farthest from the bull. Like refugees from a house on fire we rushed out.

Something in the doorway tripped me up and I went flat, one hand on a thistle and the other in a cowpat. I struggled up again, gathering my nightie up over my knees and staggered on to the edge of the beck.

In we went, not heeding its depth or temperature. Stumbling amongst the slippery stones and soaked to our knees, we struggled to the opposite bank, climbed out and raced across the field, heedless of the bog and the thistles, until we reached the wall. It was six foot high but we seemed to go over like feathers and it was not until we were safely on the other side that at last we stopped and looked back.

The bull, to our surprise, had not given chase, but was now standing guard over what remained of our encampment, holding our food, clothing and all means of support, to ransom, while we were here, alone, helpless and in our nightdresses. We began to make our way up the hillside, in a vague kind of way.

Then we began to run. There, on the top of the hill, was our deliverer, heaven sent, a man! It was the landlord of the Craven Heifer and he was rapidly disappearing out of sight. We rushed towards him, shouting and waving, quite oblivious of our unusual attire. He stopped and looked round, a little surprised, as well he might be. Fortunately, for us, as well as being the landlord of the Craven Heifer he was also a farmer. Also he had a large stick and plenty of panache. We told him what had happened.

'Wait here,' he told us. He leapt over the wall and advanced towards the bull, shouting and waving his arms.

The bull put down his head and snorted. He backed away a few yards and then started advancing towards our rescuer. We held our breath.

'Whack!' his stick came down across the bull's nose.
The bull snorted.

Our hero shouted and whacked him again.

He pawed the ground and snorted again, but came no nearer.

Our brave friend took a step closer, brandishing his stick.

The bull turned and began to retreat, slowly at first and then faster as the landlord's threats and shouts began to catch up with him. He reached the beck and, snorting and blowing most angrily, splashed his way across it.

'Come on!' shouted our bold rescuer. 'Come and get your

things before he comes back.'

In half a minute we were over the wall and haring across the field. With as near the speed of light as we could manage we tore up the tent pegs and threw everything on to the canvas of the collapsed tent: shoes, frying pan, toothbrushes, eggs, clothes, candles, bread, soap, all in a jumble. Mary took one end and I the other and we dragged the whole lot over the grass towards the wall, one eye on the bull all the time.

With considerable difficulty we heaved it shoulder high and over the wall, into a bog on the other side. As we scrambled after it we saw the bull returning through the beck, coming in our direction.

The landlord went back to the attack once more in a final show of bravado, while we set to, to drag our egg-covered garments from the heap in order to dress ourselves decently. We spent the next hour washing everything and restoring order as far as it was possible. At last the tent was up again and we had breakfast cooking by 10.30.

We were in the middle of enjoying the bacon and eggs that we had thought we should never taste again when I remembered that Alice's best pink Morny soap was in the beck, where we had all washed the night before. I remembered also that no one had cleared up the remains of our fire nor replaced the turves we had cut.

I volunteered to make the expedition to put all to rights and to retrieve the soap.

The bull was nowhere to be seen as I climbed the wall and made my way back to the camp site, but, as I was throwing the firestones back into the beck, I heard a shout from the direction of the farmhouse. It was one of the cowmen.

'Watch out!' he shouted across the valley. 'The bull'll be after you if you stay there!'

17

The ice had gone at last and we had moved the boat on another ten miles and moored somewhere on the London side of Warwick. My crew was to join me on Sunday and I spent Saturday night alone.

About three o'clock in the morning I was woken by a bright light shining throught the window of the bow cabin where I slept. I sat up in my bunk and stared out into the darkness.

'Are you Miss Radbourne?'*

'No,' I replied and turned away from the light without opening my eyes.

I must be still asleep, I thought, and having a queer kind of *Alice in Wonderland* dream, but I did not seem to wake up any more and the light continued to shine mercilessly into the cabin. I could vaguely see the silhouettes of the two figures on the bank.

'Would you please go away,' I said. 'I want to go to sleep.'

The figures muttered to each other and the torch played a brilliant beam of light across my bunk.

'We are the police,' one of them said.

'I don't care if you are the Queen,' I said to myself. 'Just go away and leave me in peace.'

'We've got your car at the station,' the voice went on. 'We found it abandoned.'

I climbed out of the bunk and stuck my head out into the cool night air. The starry sky and the black water made the whole thing even more unreal.

'Abandoned!' I cried. 'What nonsense! And why on earth

*An attempt at the author's maiden name.

do you have to come and tell me in the middle of the night?'

'Your mother wants to know if you are all right.'

'Oh!' I said. That, of course, explained everything.

I am never surprised at anything my mother does, from writing personal letters to the Queen to entertaining gypsies in the drawing room.

'Of course I'm all right,' I said.

By this time I was well awake and leaning out of the cabin window trying to see the half invisible figures on the bank, while they told me the story.

They had apparently found my car, which I had carefully parked in the nearby lane, as close to the canal as I could get. For some reason they had forced it open and driven it away. Somewhere inside they had found an envelope with my family home address on it and had rung up the local police. They, in turn, had rung up my mother, telling her that my car had been found abandoned outside a cemetery. She, not surprisingly, had told them to find out as quickly as possible whether or not I was already in the cemetery and, if so, to send her word.

I never seemed to have much luck with cars, I thought, as I set off next morning to the police station to collect mine out of pawn. This one had not been so bad, but the first one I had part-owned with Mary suffered from serious trouble in its gearbox. It went all right in first, third, top and reverse, but it did not like second at all and could only be persuaded to stay in it when I stuck my knee under the gear lever. This is what really got me through my driving test. I think the examiner was so sorry for me that he did not notice all my mistakes. I am sure it was not my knee that distracted him.

The car I had after that was ten years old when I bought it. It had had so many owners that the log book had run into a second volume. Gradually its parts fell off, one by one. The essential ones were either replaced at some cost or tied on again with string. This was in the days before MOT.

After I had had it for six months and it was back at the garage being repaired for the umpteenth time I discovered that the chassis was not only cracked but twisted. It had,

121

apparently, been in an accident. When it was straightened out I found that the steering was permanently lopsided, and from then onwards I had to drive doing a continuous left-hand-down on the steering wheel in order to keep a straight course.

Starting the car on a cold morning was a major operation. Each night, when I got home, I spent a good half an hour wrapping it up, for, until I had saved up enough to have a garage, it had to stand outside.

First, I lit an oil lamp which I hung under the bonnet. Then I covered the engine with layers of sacks, old coats and pieces of carpet. I then slammed down the bonnet, which immediately put the lamp out, so I started all over again. By this time it was usually dark and often raining, or snowing, as well.

When at last the lamp was going again and the bonnet safely shut I threw an old rug over the whole thing and topped that with an enormous heavy tarpaulin which I could barely lift. Then, for safety's sake, I piled four or five bricks on top to stop the entire contraption from blowing away.

Undoing it all in the morning took twice as long, since it was all either soaking wet and impossibly heavy, frozen stiff or buried in snow. When it was all too much I begged help from my next door neighbour, Mr Black. He took off the layers of bedding and then, while I sat inside to steer, he pushed from the back.

On icy mornings, or muddy mornings – and it was usually one or the other – the wheels spun round and round until, with a sudden jerk, they broke through the ice or got a grip on the firm ground below the mud. When this happened the car shot forward, sending Mr Black flat on his face.

After a year with this old car I realised that the repairs were costing me about twice as much as I had paid for it and I decided to sell it. Then I began to think about the poor mug who was going to buy it. The more I thought about him – I could not possibly have sold it to a her – the sorrier I felt for him and the more my conscience spoke up.

'Well, if you do find anyone silly enough to buy it,' it said to me 'you'll have to say what's wrong with it.'

This seemed to me to be a hopeless situation, an estimate which was confirmed when plenty of people came to see it and went quickly away.

At last, one Sunday morning, one of them did not go hastily away after the first look. Instead, he gave it a fairly thorough examination and then took it for a drive. I did not have to point out what was wrong with the steering; it was quite evident, but he did not raise any objections and said he would buy it.

When I saw that he was serious I got thoroughly worried and began telling him all the other things that were wrong with it, but it seemed to make no difference. I even pleaded with him to go away and think about it, but the more I tried to dissuade him the more sure he seemed to be that he wanted it. At last I gave up, thinking: 'Be it on your own head, then.' He took out his cheque book and opened it on the bonnet of the car and paid me on the spot. I took the cheque and disappeared hastily before disaster occurred. The ominous noises faded into the distance as he drove away up the lane. I never saw him again.

18

To travel by canal is to discover a whole new countryside of unknown villages and forgotten places. The waterways strike their own way through England, linking the great cities, but their journey is quite different from the route taken by roads. The villages, and even important places where one canal joins or leaves another, are almost unknown beyond the world of canals and most of them are still as they were when the navvies completed their work on the new 'navigation'.

As we travelled on towards London we passed small hamlets, undiscovered by motorists, where the working boats tied. Here, in the waterside inns, where the boats would often be moored at the end of the garden, the boatmen met and exchanged news of the canal and its traffic. The canal, to them, was something like an elongated village; the gossip travelled up and down at a similar speed. When we went ashore to fill our tanks from the water taps on the bank, or to fill ourselves with welcome beer, we found that the news of our coming had gone well ahead of us.

Braunston is a grey village which slides down a steep hill to the waterside, where a farm, a group of stone cottages and a long, low thatched inn lie on either side of the canal. Here there is a dry dock and a group of large sheds where boats are built and where, at the time of our journey, one old man still decorated the boatmen's water cans with the traditional clusters of roses. The village lies on the Birmingham side of the longest tunnel on the Grand Union. The dark entry into the hillside opens out a few yards beyond the lock.

This was about the midway mark of our journey and one sunny morning in February we passed under the roadbridge into the wide basin outside the boat sheds. Hugh was steering. He had slowed down the engine ready to enter the lock ahead of us. Suddenly he found that there was no response from the rudder. Unable to steer, we drifted helplessly across the broad stretch of water, away from the lock and into the bank.

'What's the matter?' Geoffrey called.

Hugh leaned over the stern of the boat and looked down, as far as he could, into the dark water behind.

'I think we've lost the propeller.'

The propeller was phosphor-bronze and was an expensive item to drop in the cut. While the men pulled the boat in to the bank and made her fast Madeleine and I climbed over the roof to the bows and jumped ashore. We made our way into the boatyard to see if we could borrow something to try to fish it out.

The boatmen lent us an old sixty foot hull and two twenty foot rakes. Using the rakes as punting poles we manoeuvred ourselved out into the middle of the basin to where we thought the propeller might have dropped off, then, returning the rakes to their proper use, we began to drag the bed of the canal. Backwards and forwards we worked, from bank to bank, raking and scraping. After about half an hour we hit something.

'Got it!' cried Madeleine.

'Steady now, here it comes.' Slowly she pulled the heavy rake towards her. The long prongs broke the surface and very carefully we both drew it close to the boat. We had caught the remains of an old bicycle.

Down went the rakes again, scratching and scraping and stirring up the mud, to make the water even more impenetrable than it was before. Ten minutes later we brought up an old brick, then a tin pail, a wooden box, some more bricks and a cow's skull. For two hours we wove across and across the canal, until the light began to fade and we had to give up.

☆　　☆　　☆

Next day I was recounting the story in the BBC canteen.

'Why not ask the frogmen?' someone suggested.

I did not even know, at that time, that frogmen could be found in an unlikely place like London, but I soon found that there were several sub aqua clubs and a telephone call to one of them was immediately fruitful. They would love to help and promised that someone would be along to Braunston the following Sunday morning.

I spent Saturday night alone, except for Samson, on the propeller-less boat, tied just outside the tunnel. I was up in good time next morning to be ready for the frogmen. I imagined that two or three enthusiasts would turn up and, sure enough, just before midday, I saw a small group of people coming along the towpath towards the boat.

First came a couple; then three more; then a group of five or six, then another group of about the same size. They were followed after an interval, by some stragglers who, in turn, were followed at a little distance by another half dozen. Beyond them again I could see more, and yet more. A great crowd seemed to be approaching down the towpath. In fact, the entire club had arrived, with most of their friends and relations. They swarmed on to the boat like locusts. It went down several measureable inches.

I had prepared to make tea for two or three and to provide some privacy for them to change. What was I going to do with all this lot? I told the divers that they could use the living cabin to change into their kit as it was the largest space available. I went into the galley to make some tea, wondering how I could make my half-dozen mugs go round everybody.

In a few minutes they emerged, fully clad in rubber suits, flipper feet and oxygen masks and hung around with enormous weights, as though ready to explore a Spanish wreck. They flapped along the towpath until they came to the place where I thought the propeller had dropped off. Then, with great care, they lowered themselves into the chilly, brown canal.

The water came just above their knees. One of them had a length of line and this they stretched across the canal and then, one by one, they went under. Thirty seconds after the mass submergence the head of one of them appeared

126

above the surface.

'It's murky down there,' he said, and disappeared once more.

The crowd on the towpath watched the affair with great interest. Most of Braunston village had joined the visitors by now and it looked as though they were waiting for the start of the Boat Race. I stood amongst the crowd, watching hopefully for my lost propeller to appear.

A few minutes later another frogman surfaced. He was holding something above his head. I craned my neck over the crowd to see what it was. It was one of the bricks we had fished up the weekend before. In a little while up came the tin pail, the bicycle, some more bricks and the cow's skull.

It was very cold in the February wind and I decided I would take Samson for a walk, as it looked as though the search would go on for a long time. I started to walk up the towpath and, just as I was turning on to the road I heard a shout. I looked back. One of the frogmen was emerging from the water, covered in mud, with my propeller in his arms.

Everybody crowded round, while I took a photograph of the historic moment. Then the team flapped out on to the bank, dripping and smelly and made their way back to the boat to change.

Fortunately there was a dry dock at Braunston, the only one between Birmingham and Bull's Bridge, many miles further on, and there the boat went, to have the propeller put on again. Fortunately, also, we had not travelled another quarter of a mile. If we had, the propeller would have dropped off in the darkness of Braunston's mile-long tunnel, where even Jacques Cousteau might have had trouble in finding it.

Braunston was one of the last places on the waterways where traditional roses and castles were painted on the working boats and on the cans and dippers that were carried by every boat until British Waterways, in their unimaginable wisdom, replaced them by their quick, cheap coats of blue and yellow.

While waiting for the frogmen to arrive I had paid a visit to Sam Barlow's yard at Braunston to see the old man who did the painting. I found him in the paint room, the floor and walls splashed with bright scarlet, yellow, blue and green. He was putting the last touches of brilliant colour to a water can.

'Can I buy one?' I enquired.

He nodded.

'How much?'

'Eh, I don't know, rightly. There is a list somewhere but I don't know where he is.'

'Can you find it for me?' I asked. 'I'll be here again next weekend.'

The following Saturday I sought him out again.

'Have you found out how much the cans are?' I asked.

'Well, no, I can't find the list,' he replied, 'But I'll get 'e for you.'

The third weekend came.

'Yes, I've got 'e for you now,' he told me. 'Here 'tis, somewhere. Aye. They're thirty shillings each. Far too much 'tis. I remembers when they was four and sixpence, and we gave a beer mug with 'em as well.'

Sadly, I never bought one. I had more urgent uses for thirty shillings at that time and I did not know how soon such things would cease to be used and become collectors' pieces.

At last the repair on the boat was done and we were ready to set off once more. From the dry dock *The Chester* was launched back into the canal and we headed towards London once again. Immediately, we entered the mile-long tunnel beneath the hill which rose high above Braunston village to the south.

The darkness was complete. Christopher lit the Tilley lamp and went through the length of the boat to the forward cabin and climbed out through the window. Holding a mackintosh cape round his shoulders he crouched on the little deck, while the light of the lamp cast a queer glow over the inky water and lit up the arching brick walls and roof.

The rest of us were all on the aft deck, peering into the darkness as well as we could and hoping we would not meet another boat in the narrow channel.

Slowly we chugged on, the sound of the engine echoing off the tunnel walls. Water dropped in cascades over us through holes over our heads. We turned up our collars. The cold was intense and it was impossible to hear one another's voices above the noise of the engine. I thought of the boatmen of the earlier days who legged their boats through the tunnels while the horses were led over the top of the hill to resume their towing on the far side of the tunnel. They would have done it in silence as well as darkness; no light from a Tilley lamp, and only the lapping of the water between the boat sides and the wall, water into which they could, and did, so easily slip, probably to be crushed by the weight of their own boat before they could climb back on board.

The loud throbbing and the unchanging darkness and the sudden falls of cold water, made us lose all sense of time. We seemed to have been underground for an age when, at last, at the far end of the tunnel, appeared a pinpoint of silver light.

It seemed impossible that we should ever get through it. Slowly it grew to a circle of silver and, as we crept towards it, at barely a walking pace, it spread its circumference wider and wider until, at length, we saw the trees and hedges reflected in a perfect circle in its still half and came out into the sunshine again.

19

April came. The ice dropped out of the wind and we shed out top layers of jackets and pullovers.

By now we had become skilful in our handling of the boat. We rarely found ourselves on the mud now. We had the routine of working through the locks well under control and had reduced our time to six minutes to get through a lock that was ready for us. The working boats took an average of four minutes so we felt we were really to be congratulated. Now we were able to enjoy the spells of peace between one lock and another, when we could watch the quiet fields glide gently by and look with appreciation at the curves of the old stone bridges and eighteenth century lock cottages, until a shout from the helmsman – 'Lock coming!' – brought us all up on deck, at the ready for the activity of working through.

When there was a flight of locks, leading one out of another, or with short pounds between, there would be no pause for perhaps several hours, as lock after lock was filled and opened, ropes coiled, thrown and tied around bollards, paddles opened and closed and crew jumped on and off. When, at last, the final lock gates opened to a level stretch of water we relaxed again, prepared and ate meals and talked.

By this stage we were so much in control of the situation that we could plan our day to have a midday stop at a canalside pub. These forgotten inns of the waterways are, or were, known to few beyond the people of the canals. They are often down some country lane which leads nowhere, even in the industrial Midlands. Here, in the evenings, the boat people met and exchanged news. Without post or radio they kept in touch with all that was going on. News passed up and down the narrow ways by its own strange means. Everyone, we found, knew that we were coming and where we were going. Every boat was known individually and, even after conversion would seem to alter it beyond all knowledge, it could still be recognized. On my final mooring I was sitting on the roof in the sunshine one day when a working boat quietly throbbed its way past.

'Is that one of Jacob ....'s boats?' the boatman called to me.

'I don't know,' I called back. 'It came from the Severn Run, from Gloucester to Stourport.'

'I know,' he shouted back, almost past by now. 'It's an old Severner, one of Jacob's boats. I recognize it.'

Spring came in the span between one weekend and the next. The trees, bare a week ago, were suddenly frothed with delicate green. Willows in canalside gardens trailed their long fingers in the water; horse-chestnut buds were fat and ready to burst into flower; every tree and bush, every field, wore the ethereal green which vanishes like a dream at the heavy touch of summer.

We were followed by swans and dippers. Rounding a bend one early morning we came upon two swans close to each other on their nests. Their mates, standing nearby, rose up, stretched their necks menacingly towards us, then arched their wings and clapped them over their backs. A hare of enormous size loped across a field and three cuckoos flew, calling, across the water.

With the coming of the sun everything seemed to go more smoothly. Only Samson continued to become involved in difficulties. He had made a habit of jumping ashore as soon as we entered a full lock, where the water level was up to the lock side, but it had not really registered with him that when he was ready to jump on board again, the boat was not where he had left it. He looked at the lock where it had been with the air of confused surprise as if saying:

'There was a boat there just now, I know. I was on it. Blessed thing's gone.'

131

Eventually he would look down into the lock and recognize the roof of the boat, perhaps eight or ten feet below him. He would then look round in pained surprise at his plight.

The boat was ready to move out of the lock by this time and the gates about to open. In the minutes remaining to us we attempted to coax him to jump, at the same time trying to keep the boat from drifting across the lock away from him. When he saw the widening gap between himself and the boat he did at last realize that he would have to get over to the other side, across the top of the lock gates. He usually left this to the very last minute so that the gates were actually opening as he made his leap across, in the path of our oncoming bows. I suffered minor nervous breakdowns on each occasion.

Sometimes he failed to get on board again at all. When this happened he ran along the towpath beside us, usually on the side farthest away from us, barking loudly, until we were able to draw in to the bank and take him on board.

On one occasion he misjudged the distance and fell into the none too clean water. He turned back towards the bank and tried to scramble out, but the bank was too steep and he sank back and disappeared under the water. I watched him vanish with horror but no one else showed the least concern. A moment later we saw him heading quite happily for the opposite bank, where he scrambled out without any difficulty, soaked and evil smelling. We kept our course and did not invite him on board until the last possible moment.

One Sunday morning we had just passed through a lock and, as usual, Samson had been left behind. He followed us, running and barking madly along the bank. There was no towpath on the side where he was. Fields and gardens came right down to the water's edge. Samson raced across the first field and leapt the fence, to find himself in someone's garden. The owner was having a quiet Sunday morning dig. He looked up, considerably annoyed. Geoffrey, in the meantime, had spotted that there was not just one garden, but a whole series of them, side by side. He leapt ashore and gave chase.

His fence jumping was nearly as good as Samson's and from the boat we had a ringside view of him, leaping fence

132

after fence and waving and calling apologies, as he pursued Samson through smallholdings and orchards, scattering chickens and cats, bowing and smiling apologetically to a succession of very surprised onlookers.

At last Samson vanished altogether, apparently under the canal. From the boat we watched the comic procession, not sure whether to laugh or wring our hands, until a few minutes later they both emerged on the towpath side of the canal, having apparently discovered some kind of subterranean alleyway.

There was a third tunnel on the journey, at Blisworth. This was nearly two miles long. We entered it in total blackness, for it has a twist and the far end, with its star of light, was not visible until two thirds of the journey was over. Fortunately no other boat was coming in the opposite direction and we reached the end in safety.

We had just finished working through the next lock and were loosing the ropes from the bollards when we saw a young man running down the towpath towards us.

'Can I come on board?' he said.

We saw no reason why not and helped him across the widening gap of water on to the small deck. He had a camera slung round his neck and soon announced that he was a press photographer. He did his best to extract the story of our journey from us, but we did not tell him.

There were now nine of us on board and we took it in turns to laze in the sun on the roof. Shouts of 'Bridge coming!' from the helmsman sent us all flat on our faces to avoid being scraped off, which seemed to amuse the lines of Sunday strollers who gathered overhead to watch us pass.

We had just left Leighton Buzzard one quiet Sunday morning. All was going well, in contrast to the days of January and February, and we were all enjoying the experience. Suddenly I noticed a smell of burning. It was coming from the engine hole. Quickly we pulled up the hatches. Out shot a cloud of smoke, followed by tongues of flame. We leapt backwards and forwards on the tiny deck, falling into one another in our anxiety to put out the fire. At last Hugh spotted the trouble. When the engine was closed down for the night we always covered it with a green canvas tarpaulin. This had not been removed when the engine was started up that morning, and was now on fire. Hugh took hold of one corner and Christopher grabbed the other and together they hauled it up and out of the engine hole. They dropped it over the side; the water hissed as the flames died and we chugged on, leaving the tarpaulin to sink below the surface behind us.

☆   ☆   ☆

We had not taken any water on board since the journey started and, indeed, I was fairly hazy about the important matter of providing myself with enough water for normal living.

There were two storage tanks in the galley and water came into them through yards and yards of black hosepipe. One end of the pipe had to be attached to a standpipe somewhere on the bank and the other was pushed into a hole in the side of the boat which led, eventually, into the header tank. After that, a series of cocks had to be opened, all in the right order, and when that was done water ran through the header tank into a large storage tank below. When, eventually, I had to do the job on my own it proved quite formidable.

The first task was to open all the cocks, then I had to turn on the water. The standpipe was usually some distance from the boat and by the time I got back from turning on the water, if all had gone well, there was a sound of gurgling as the tanks filled up. Generally, however, I returned to the boat to find either the end of the hosepipe hanging over the side and water pouring in through the open window, or, if I had miscalculated the amount left in the tank, the galley floor would be awash from end to end.

The storage tank filled up first and there was a hatch over it which could be removed so that one could watch it fill. It was difficult to gauge the moment when it was full as it was quite dark inside. It was usually done by means of a wooden spoon, used as a dipstick. The moment the tank was full the cock had to be turned off so that no more ran into the tank but was diverted to the header tank. The storage tank took about three quarters of an hour to fill and it usually happened that, at the critical moment, when I was bent over it, gazing into its depths, someone would arrive. My attention being diverted for a second, the water, which until then had shown no sign of reaching the top, poured over in a flood and at the same moment the cock jammed. Water went merrily running all over the floor until I could get the cock turned off to divert it into the header tank. This happened every week.

There was no way of knowing when the header tank was full. All one could do was to listen to the note of the water, as it changed from 'splosh splosh splosh' to 'splash splash splash'. The moment it became 'splish splish splish' it was necessary to run at full speed up the companionway steps, jump ashore, run to the tap and turn it off, at top speed. If one was not impeded by pedestrians, mooring lines, dogs, visitors arriving and families of swans and cygnets on the bank, it could be done just in time to prevent disaster, but the smallest hitch produced a further flood, which could be all over the floor by the time I got back. Needless to say, I soon learned to cut down my weekly consumption of water.

At my final mooring place the standpipe was situated by the lock, about two hundred yards from the boat and on the opposite side of the canal. To fill the tanks I had to move the boat up to the lock, pull her across the canal and tie her as close to the pipe as possible. On a summer morning it was pleasant to sit on the roof of the boat in the sunshine and listen to the varying sounds of the running water and carry on a conversation with the fishermen on the bank, but in the winter it was another matter. The short evenings frequently caught me on the wrong side of the canal, waiting in the dark for the tanks to fill. Then came the hazardous journey back to my mooring place. It was not worth starting the engine, of course, even if I could have done it, so I had to punt the boat with a twenty foot pole. I climbed on the roof, trying to keep my balance with the pole in my hands. Then I pushed off from the bank, anxiously listening for the sound of an approaching boat which could run me down in the dark.

One good push sent the boat well out across the water,

completely blocking the canal with her seventy feet of length. The heavy pole was far from easy to manage. When it slipped through my hands it filled them with splinters and I was constantly in danger of losing my balance and sliding into the water.

As soon as the bows touched the bank on the mooring side I ran along the top of the roof, holding the pole horizontally like an acrobat on the high wire, but not so confidently. Then, with the bow line in my hand I leapt ashore and pulled her hard in to the bank.

Occasionally, if I was lucky, I had a friend who could hold the stern line and together we inched her down the bank to her mooring place. On a calm day this was reasonably easy and, provided we got the rope round the bow post and pulled her in hard, all was well, but in wind it was difficult and quite dangerous since she was not only long but very heavy, being built of solid oak.

One night I was bringing her back in total darkness. A strong wind was blowing straight across the canal so that we could not hold the boat. The ropes slipped through our wet hands and, caught by the wind, she swung out into the centre of the canal in a wide arc. I felt she might go altogether. I dug my heels in, took a firmer grip on the rope, bending my small weight against it. Slowly she began to respond and to swing back towards the bank. We pulled in the slack of the rope. Then I realized that she had moved beyond the mooring place and the line on which she was swinging back was bringing her directly on to the boat on the next mooring, a twenty foot lifeboat conversion. With the wind behind her my boat would almost certainly crush the smaller boat against the bank.

At that moment I heard the sound of a step on the path behind me. It was impossible to see who it was, in the darkness, but whoever it was, the owner of the feet must also have a pair of hands.

I shouted through the wind: 'Get this rope round a tree. Quick!'

The owner of the feet jumped immediately to the situation, as boat people always do. Slowly my boat came under control and began to move gently back towards us and into her own mooring place. I shouted my thanks through the darkness as the feet continued on their way and disappeared.

Another problem was getting fuel on board. The two fires on the boat seemed to need enormous quantities and I was hard put to it to keep them supplied. At first I brought sackfuls from my parents' home, in the car and lumped them on my back over the top of the lock gates, which was the only approach to the mooring. Later on the lock keeper allowed me to have coal and coke delivered to his back yard and from there I carried the loads over in sacks once or twice a week.

The top of the lock gates was narrow and the water deep. It rushed in quite a frightening way through the leaking paddles below. Holding the low handrail with one hand and steadying the rocking sack on my shoulder with the other, I inched my way across in some fear of losing my balance.

I was not helped by Samson. He would weave up and down the bank, sniffing industriously, until I had reached a point about halfway across, usually at the place where the two gates met, where there could often be a gap to negotiate as well. Then, without warning, he would leap on to the gate and charge his way across, under and between my legs.

Then I was given a coracle. This was an excellent, if alarming, means of transport. Bobbing about in this shopping basket of a boat, loaded with sacks of coal, I made my uncertain way across the canal, praying that no working boats would appear until I had reached the other side. I was never actually run down, though I occasionally came near to being entangled in their tow ropes.

Visitors were always anxious to try their skill with the coracle. They felt sure it must be quite easy and usually ended by falling in. I was more fortunate or less adventurous and never did more than get my feet wet.

☆　　☆　　☆

I had been promised a mooring near Chiswick bridge but we never reached it.

A week before I should have moored there I went to confirm the arrangements. The site was owned by a middle-aged woman who lived on one of the boats. In response to

137

my knock she put her head out of the hatch.

'You remember I came here some time ago about a mooring for my narrowboat?' I reminded her.

She looked me up and down without speaking, for a moment or two, and then: 'I haven't any moorings left,' she said.

I was too stunned to argue and, in any case, I had absolutely no evidence that she had promised me a mooring, and I saw that she would not be in the least concerned if I told her that my boat was even now on its way, with nowhere to go at the end of the journey.

'Something will happen,' I told myself as cheerfully as I could, but the thought of starting the despairing search all over again, gave me a heavy heart. I walked away from the moorings in a state of deep gloom and hopelessness.

I returned to the boat the following weekend and we moved her on again until we were within eighteen miles of London. On the Sunday evening we passed through a lock on the far side of Uxbridge and tied the boat to the bank just below. There were four other boats moored there on a peaceful stretch of water lined by high beeches. We threw out the mooring lines and stopped the engine. Its insistent chugging ceased in an almost palpable silence. The water lapped quietly and then grew still around the boat.

We did not know it, but our five months' journey was over.

We had discovered another world, removed from this day by a century and in spirit by an age, a world where time has another meaning. Life slows to a healing pace, bringing tranquility.

Perhaps the waterways are the last place left in England where peace can be found, where there is still courtesy and friendliness. This sense of timelessness remains, even at rest. Here, on my mooring the water scarcely moves, except when a boat passes. Its still surface perfectly reflects the great trees that line the bank, and the sky beyond. The beauty of sunrise and sunset is repeated in the water. Swans glide gently past. Squirrels run up and down the trees. A heron stands motionless beside the towpath, still as a tree stump, silently watching.

The quiet is broken by a rush of water and the rattle of paddles being dropped at the lock as a pair of painted boats work through, loaded deep in the water or riding high, a line of washing in the empty hold. The sun strikes the brilliance of the brass chimney ring. A child tied to the cabin roof plays with a caged bird. The boatman at his rudder and his wife on the butty nod a greeting as they pass, unhurried and tranquil.

My mooring lines tug and tighten and the wash of the boats laps against the hull and dies away in the bank. The boats vanish through the bridge. The mooring lines relax. A squirrel flashes along a branch and is gone. Stillness returns.